I0677450

GOLDMAKER

A MODERN ALCHEMIST

A SUSPENSE THRILLER BY

JAMES M. HUGHES

Award-winning author of *The Baja Project* and *The Cuban Affair*

No part of this publication may be reproduced
in whole or in part, or stored in a retrieval system,
or transmitted in any form or by any means,
electronic, mechanical, photocopying, recording,
or otherwise, without written permission of the author,
except for the inclusion of brief quotations in a review.
For information regarding permission, please write to:
info@barringerpublishing.com

Copyright © 2012 James M. Hughes
All rights reserved.

Barringer Publishing, Naples, Florida
www.barringerpublishing.com
Cover, graphics, layout design by Lisa Camp
Editing by Carole Greene

ISBN: 978-0-9882034-0-2

Library of Congress Cataloging-in-Publication Data
Goldmaker / James M. Hughes

Printed in U.S.A.

This is a work of fiction. All characters, organizations,
and events portrayed in this novel are either products of the
author's imagination or are used fictitiously.

AUTHOR'S NOTE

I thank the readers of my first two novels who encouraged me to write a third. As with my previous stories, historical facts and places are accurate. It is the intertwining of those facts and places, and adding an icing of imagination, that makes fiction. Why write these stories? To become William Abbey, Professor Brenda Johnson, or Agent Kate Mackie and travel the world of action and adventure with them. A reader becomes engrossed in a good story. The writer lives it for far longer than a single read. One reader asked about my first book, *The Baja Project,* "Is this a true story?" My answer to that question remains the same for each of my books: "It could be."

PROLOGUE

FIFTEEN YEARS AGO, IN BOSTON

The secretary gestured toward the closed door behind her desk. "The president is expecting you, Professor Conan. Go right in."

Henry Conan lifted his shoulders to stretch his full five-and-a-half feet and reached up to straighten the tie he had quickly borrowed when summoned by the president. His shoes had half-inch lifts in the heels, and, as usual, creased pants broke a bit long on top of them. They made him look taller, a tailor had once told him. Though short, Conan was a handsome man with a square jaw and close-cropped black hair.

He noticed the secretary didn't rise to show him in, which caused a tweak of concern, but he was expecting good news. There had been rumors that he was on track for an early tenure vote. Maybe this was the announcement. Could even be a chair in the physics department. Some had called him a child prodigy. Since childhood, he had known that he was smarter than most, but it was hard work and a laser focus that had propelled him into academic life. Rarely did he lose that focus. Even now, he grinned as he pictured the first step of the goal almost in hand. He was Professor Henry David Conan. In Boston, where his namesake, Henry

David Thoreau, had written more than a century ago, he expected to live up to his name.

Conan opened the door and walked into the office, hearing a click as the door shut behind him. President Graves was seated behind a polished oak desk with the Charles River flowing dark and gray outside his window. Conan had met the president a number of times but never in his office.

"Mr. President," Conan spoke as he strode toward the desk, but he stopped abruptly when he saw the expression on the man's face.

The older man looked up with a frown, rested his chin on the heel of his hand, and sighed. His eyebrows were raised and his lips pressed together as he shook his head slowly from side to side.

"Henry, how…how could you have sex with the dean's secretary, who, I believe, is married, and twenty years your senior? On the couch in the dean's office! Why would you do that?" The president grimaced. "Why…she could be your mother!"

Professor Conan froze in place. *Two days, he thought. It took her only two days to talk. There goes our little secret. But I got the book!*

"Sir…sir, I—I can explain." His mind was racing. *I can't really explain. I can't mention the book.*

Only a week ago, he had glimpsed the ancient journal—small and leather bound—high on a shelf in the dean's office. The title, in Latin, had been barely visible from where he had stood. He knew it translated to *Alchemy Solved*, and he also knew the author, Jehova Sanctus Unus— The Great One—the secret pseudonym of the famous Sir Isaac Newton. Among his better-known accomplishments, Newton had been the leading alchemist of the seventeenth century. Alchemy, the quest for gold, had been Professor Conan's passion and goal since childhood. He'd heard of this book, but most alchemists thought it had disappeared over the centuries. As soon as he saw it, he knew he had to have it.

Two days ago, at a faculty cocktail party, he found himself talking to the dean's assistant, Irene. They had been friends since he joined the university. She shared plenty of welcome advice with the new professor and always stood ready to lend a helping hand. A few glasses of wine, and the plan popped into his mind.

"Irene, can you give me a private showing of the dean's office?"

"Why would you want that, Henry?" she flashed back with a sloppy smile and unfocused eyes. She was older but she had a good smile, good teeth. He had always preferred older women with good teeth. They brought back thoughts of his mother.

"I've seen that she has an amazing collection of rare physics books." He leaned in with more of a whisper—their secret. "I can't really ask her to browse around her bookshelves. But I'd love to do just that!" He squeezed her arm slightly. "You could do it…"

She whispered back, "Well, I'm not sure. The building's all locked…"

"I'm sure you have keys, Irene. You can get us in." He looked over his shoulder then turned to her conspiratorially. "A little adventure—our little adventure. No one's going to care. Come on, let's have an adventure."

He finally convinced her, and they left the party and walked furtively to the dean's office. Once inside the dimly lit office, he gazed up at the bookcase and drew her closer. One thing led to another. First they kissed, tentatively; then they touched and excited each other. He hadn't planned on it going so far—he just wanted to get the book—but he realized it was a useful diversion.

"Oh, Henry, we really shouldn't," she protested as she folded back onto the couch with him sprawled on top of her. Soon his pants were off and her skirt lifted.

She asked tentatively, "Do you have…?"

"Protection? Yes, of course. I have a condom."

"I might need…" She closed her eyes and whispered, "Lubrication."

"It's okay. It's lubricated, and I can help you."

Afterward, she asked in a trembling voice, "Have you ever done it…from…behind?"

"I think I know how. Get on your knees and lean down on your elbows," he coaxed. "You'll have to help guide me in."

"There…oh, Henry. There…it's right there! Oh my god, that's wonderful!"

He withdrew. "I'll get a towel," he whispered in her ear. He found one in the adjacent bathroom, and on his way back, he climbed onto a chair and grabbed the cherished book from the top shelf, folding it into his jacket so Irene wouldn't see it. *I bet the dean will never miss it,* he thought as he hurried back. *Probably doesn't even know it's there.*

"Let's keep this our little secret," he whispered as he returned to the couch.

She was standing and took a deep breath as she straightened her clothes, her eyes cast down. "Oh, yes, it's our secret, Professor Conan. I'm so embarrassed. We went too far. I…I had too much wine. I've never done anything like this before."

"Don't worry, Irene. Just think of it as a one-time fling. No one else needs to know."

He jolted alert in front of the president's desk. They certainly knew now. Two days! He had to say something. He swallowed hard, trying to find his voice. "We just had a little too much wine and got carried away, sir. Nothing to do with the school or our work. Just a social indiscretion." *How much does he really know?*

"You can't be serious, Henry. Just a social indiscretion? The dean—your dean—has made it quite clear she doesn't want to set eyes on you again. You are finished here. You'll find another position. And I'll give you a glowing recommendation. But for God's sake, behave a bit better in the future. You were on the fast track for tenure. A solid physicist. And you throw it all away for a one-night fling? What in the world were you thinking?"

Conan stood stiffly, staring at the still-seated president. *I was thinking I had to get the goddamned book, but I can't tell you that. Can't let anyone know about it.*

He had already translated a small portion:

> *Sun...Sun...*
> *The rays of the sun.*
> *The heat of the sun.*
> *I need more—I need all of the sun!*

Those were Newton's cryptic words written on the last page of the journal.

Conan knew he wasn't going to find enough sun in Boston. If he was going to make gold, he had to go south. He just hadn't expected to go so soon.

He nodded, shook his head, and extended his hand. "I'm sorry it's come to this, sir. I wasn't thinking. I'll go quietly. Won't cause a stir."

CHAPTER 1
THE PRESENT, IN MIAMI

Agent Kathryn Mackie looked at the dingy sign over the doorway. *El Paisano.* She pulled to the curb and got out of her car, rolling her shoulders and stretching her neck as her eyes scanned the neighborhood. These confrontations were a bit different from protecting the President of the United States, but the President she'd guarded was no longer in office, and the Secret Service covered counterfeiting as well as presidential protection. So she had moved on to chasing bad money.

Tall and lean, she walked to the front door and pushed her sunglasses up to her forehead; it would be dark inside. She wanted to be able to see as soon as possible. She knew there'd be a bunch of scumbags inside. And they'd test her. They always did. Up till now, she'd always won. At five-feet-seven inches and 145 pounds, at least she wasn't one of the balloon-breasted, big-assed ladies these guys claimed they liked. *Isn't a matter of like, she thought. It's all they can get.*

The door was solid wood with a center pane covered by plywood, the glass behind probably broken. As she pulled the door open with one hand, screeching hinges announced her arrival. It was dark inside, and

Mackie could see very little as her pupils began to adjust to the black. She sensed eyes on her, scanning her jeans and tight sweater. She knew they'd spend more time on her breasts than her hands. She had dressed for the part.

"Señorita, would you mind staying there for a moment while my assistants make sure you carry no weapon." It was not phrased as a question; it was an order, but one she had expected. The words came from a shadowy figure seated at a table in the middle of the room. She saw a bar with stools behind him and a dozen tables scattered down each side of the room. A furtive shadow moved in front of her, and a pair of hands patted down her sides to her legs and ankles, spending more time than necessary at her breasts and crotch. She clenched her jaw in irritation.

Her vision cleared as she was pronounced clean.

"Nothing but boobs and pussy, boss. Nice ones, too."

"I apologize for his crudeness, señorita." The seated man chuckled. "Come, have a seat and we will do our business." He waved her forward with his right hand and pointed to the chair across the table from him.

She walked ten steps and sat as directed, her knees almost touching his. She could smell his cigarettes and his lunch, not pleasant smells. In the middle of the table was a one-inch pile of bills—Franklins.

"Here is my merchandise, señorita. Examine them; take your time. I think you will be pleased."

She lifted the pile of bills, fanned them with her left thumb, and pulled one from the middle. "Turn on some lights so I can see," she directed. The man waved his hand, and a bulb in an overhead ceiling fan popped on. Pulling a small loupe from her pocket, she bent down with her eyes just inches above the bill.

"My men missed that in your pocket?" the man exclaimed.

She lifted her eyes and looked at him. "I think they were too interested in the boobs and the pussy." Mackie returned to the bill.

"Well, no matter. You will see I even have the threads right, and the other markers, which are supposed to be so secret." He sat up and puffed his chest out. "A very good job, wouldn't you say?"

She lifted her eyes again. "They're okay." She paused and stared at the smelly man. "I've seen a lot worse. We'll pay a dollar a hundred."

He smiled, and in the dim light she could see his stained teeth.

"I'm not giving them away, señorita. Fifty a hundred. Half of face value—no less." He continued, "And remember, you're a lady in a room full of my friends." Raising his arms, he said, "Maybe I'll throw in a bonus for you in return for your friendship."

Her stomach turned.

He reached over and grabbed her right hand, which still held the bill. "Maybe you can be friendly to all of us…"

Mackie's left hand moved from her lap to the table, holding what looked to be a belt buckle. She leaned in and spoke softly, so only he could hear. "Tell your men to stay where they are and take your hand off of me, or this buckle, which contains a four-inch blade, will go through your neck, into your windpipe, and probably reach your brain. If it reaches your brain, you die quick. If not, you'll drown in your own blood."

He leaned back and lifted his arms in surrender, looking around the room, then at her. "Amigos, stay where you are. Do not bother the señorita." He swiveled back to Mackie. "You misunderstand my poor attempt at humor. I only joke."

"How many of these bills do you have?" she said curtly.

He answered through gritted teeth, "Three million—I have three million dollars of bills—thirty thousand bills."

"I'll pay you one million, a third of face value. That's it—the extent of my friendship."

He paused, tilted his head, and nodded. "I think we have a deal, señora." Now she was a mature woman—not a young señorita.

Mackie stood. "The money's in my car. I'll get it." Looking down, she said, "Where are the rest of the bills?"

"They'll be here when you return. They are not far—in the back room." He jerked his thumb over his shoulder.

She turned and walked to the door, which was pulled open for her. On the sidewalk, she wiped her forehead with her right hand—the prearranged signal and one she really needed, as sweat dripped into her eyes. A dozen other agents sprang from hiding and rushed the building. She moved aside as four poured in the front door, and she knew there were four more in the back and snipers perched on nearby roofs. Over the flash grenades, she heard through the bullhorn, "United States Secret Service agents! Drop all weapons and down on the floor. Face down. Now!"

Two shots rang out, quickly answered by automatic fire and a shotgun blast.

"We said down, you sons of bitches. Try that again, and you're all dead!"

A short while later, Agent Mackie sat in her car and watched the handcuffed men led from the building and hauled away in four black vans. This wasn't exactly the work she had hoped for when she moved into the presidential security detail of the Secret Service. She recalled how it had happened. After a year and a half on the detail, her sponsor, President Natalie Menton, had completed her term and decided to retire from politics. The strings which had been pulled for Mackie snapped back. She'd remained with the Secret Service but had to accept a transfer to the counterfeiting group. "To fill out your training, get you up to speed in the areas you jumped over," was the explanation. Though it was not a demotion, she understood the message. She had to put in her time as everyone else had. She didn't complain.

Agent Robert Guest had observed the operation from a dark-windowed van parked a block away. Once he saw the prisoners being taken away, he got out and walked to Mackie's car. He gestured for her to roll down the window.

"Good job, Mackie." He tapped the car door. "We got seven of them and a whole bunch of bad bills. What happened in there, anyway?"

She looked at him and smiled. "I think they underestimated me, Bob. That happens, you know. That happens a lot when you put a woman in with a bunch of men. And not only with the bad guys."

He nodded. "Message received, Special Agent. Loud and clear. You've shown you can do more than protect your friend the president." He bent down with his hands on the window edge. "And that's probably why I was just directed to give you a new assignment."

"What do you mean, a new assignment?" she shot back.

"You've been assigned to some new, hotshot task force being assembled here in Miami."

"To do what?"

"I don't know much, and I'm supposed to tell you even less." He hesitated then pointed at her left ear, which carried a gold stud. "But that's what it's about."

"What's *that*, Bob?"

"Gold, Mackie. It's about gold. Gold earrings, gold ingots, gold coins."

He straightened to leave, looking down at his agent, hands on his waist with elbows pointing out. "It's all about gold, Mackie."

CHAPTER 2
FORT MYERS, FLORIDA

Professor Conan stood at his workbench and centered the metal branding plate on top of the yellow bar. With his right hand, he swung down hard with a rubber mallet, striking one blow to impress his sign into the bar. Lifting the plate, he gazed down at his workmanship. He smiled at the circle of the sun with rays extending outward. Below the sun symbol, the purification index indicated *99.999*. Below it, the weight read *1k,* one kilogram of pure gold. He kept smiling as he thought back over the years since Boston.

President Graves had been good to his word and provided a solid recommendation for a position at another university. With that and the professor's strong academic record, a new teaching position wasn't hard to find. More difficult was finding the right location.

Newton's journal had insisted that successful transmutation of one metal to another required honoring the principles of the ancient Greek Philosopher's Stone, also called the Emerald Tablet. Those principles held that all power over matter came from the sun and was transmitted to the wind and waters below, and that only by harnessing those natural forces could the secrets of matter—and the transformation of one type of matter to another—be understood. Many modern scientists debunked such stuff as witchcraft, but Conan respected the ancient wisdom. He knew alchemy was a philosophical tradition, based as much on soft philosophy as on hard science. An alchemist needed to know formulas and theorems, but he also had to understand the essence of life. Almost all civilizations recognized that life evolved from the sun. After all, he thought, the sun was the first alchemist, converting hydrogen to helium in successive, never-ending hydrogen explosions.

He was trying to harness that power.

So Conan had looked for a place with plenty of sunlight. He wanted to remain in the United States. The sun shone most consistently in the southwest deserts, but he also needed running river water—in short supply in the dry deserts. He focused on Florida—the Sunshine State—and looked for a river, a university, and a private location. His quest soon narrowed to southwest Florida and, ultimately, to the ranch house where he now lived along the banks of the Caloosahatchee River, a few miles east of Ft. Myers and a short drive from Florida Gulf Coast University. The house was modest—twenty-five hundred square feet with two bedrooms and a large office/workshop running the full length of one side.

He had found the river water contaminated, but a filtration system solved that. A small channel off the river had been dug years ago to provide water for cattle, and the flow was easily diverted to a trough outside his workshop window facing south to the river. Another professor helped him design a filtration system to purify the river water. It took two filters: first a membrane to remove particulates, and then an ion exchange canister to neutralize the dissolved nitrogen and phosphorus. After building the filter system, he could drink the water with safety and it was pure enough for his work. Newton's words had been clear: pure water was needed.

Year after year, he did one test after another using different temperatures, different metals, different combinations of water and air. After so many experiments and so many variations, he had become frustrated and almost quit many times, but memories of his mother's pleas to work on and work hard always won out.

Now he reached over and lifted the dog-eared journal to reread the passage written inside the front cover five hundred years ago—the one that had taken him so long to understand:

Look to the sun when it's so high in the skies:
That its rays burn with brilliance and touch matter as it lies.
Look to pure water, which cools that in the mold;
A pinch of like matter turns lead into gold.

He gazed out the large window over his workbench to the scrub pines and saw grass that had once supported longhorn cattle. Today it supported three thirty-foot metal towers. Each tower was capped with a twelve-inch-diameter crystal parabolic mirror to direct the sun's rays to the window over his bench. Properly focused, the mirrors could concentrate solar rays and heat a substance well above the two-thousand-degree melting point of gold. The mirrors were an off-the-shelf item. He had built the computer-driven mounts that powered each one. The pure running water was right outside his window. Newton's short poem had been the closer. You had to do more than just heat with the sun's rays. The rays had to actually touch the metal being melted, a real embrace—not an air kiss—a real kiss.

He had needed a cover. Making gold was his private, very secret quest. So at Florida Gulf Coast University, he rewrapped his physics credentials into the science of harnessing natural forces to create energy—in particular, the heat of the sun to heat water and create steam and power. At the university, he had built a reputation for being green, but only on the surface. Professor Conan's real color was gold. That's what he was all about.

༄

On the bench was the gold bar he had poured this afternoon. It now carried his stamp—the face of the sun. One kilo, he thought. *About thirty-two ounces, worth fifty thousand dollars.*

"And I can make one every sunny day," he whispered. "More than one, if I want." He nodded as he carried the bar to the metal briefcase sitting next to a large, black iron safe. The bar fit tightly into one of the ten molded depressions in the case, the only depression still empty. He then hefted the case into the safe and spun the dial.

"Time for another shipment." He pulled out his phone to speed dial the number for Bonita Bees delivery service.

"Mr. Acme, this is Henry David.... Yes, I'm fine, thank you. I have another briefcase to be delivered. This time to Boca.... Tomorrow is fine.... A bit earlier, if possible. How about ten in the morning?... Great. Yes. Same place—Home Depot. I'll have the delivery address for the driver. I'll give him a check when I see him, and I'll return at five to get the case back from him.... Thanks. I'll call you again in a couple of weeks."

He knew the case would be a lot lighter but not completely empty when he got it back. There would be a check in it for—he hit the calculator button on his phone and multiplied—just about $498,000. This was his sixth delivery. He was close to his goal.

CHAPTER 3
FEDERAL BUILDING, MIAMI

Agent Mackie drove to the federal building as directed and asked for Mr. John Perkins after showing her badge to get through security. The guards kept her pistol, a Glock standard with a twenty-eight-round magazine of .357-caliber shells. She had never needed to use the two extra magazines she always carried.

"Just till you leave, ma'am. We'll hold it right here. The extra magazines, too."

She was alone in the elevator, wondering what was going on. Looking at her reflection in the metal doors, she patted her short hair into place and checked her lipstick. She didn't have time for much more. She hoped there would be an improvement in her assignment. She didn't really like chasing counterfeiters, but after she had joined the presidential protection arm of the Secret Service with the assistance of former President Menton, she knew she had to put in her time and not make waves. She did her job well, working as hard as any of her peers. She had come in with special treatment, and she knew there was some resentment over that, understandably. Maybe this new assignment would be a good one.

But John's comment about gold made no sense to her.

She walked off the elevator on the sixth floor and turned left as she had been directed. Five people waited for her in the room: one other woman—middle aged and dressed in a dark suit—and four men. She didn't know any of them. All were seated around a large table, reading spiral-bound reports with black covers. Five heads rose when she entered. She saw one unopened report in front of the only empty chair. Emblazoned across the cover in white letters were the words Top Secret.

"Agent Mackie, thanks for coming so quickly," spoke the man at the end of the table as he stood. "I know you were involved in a field action. Sorry to pull you in like this, but we have to move fast on this new assignment."

"I understand, sir," Mackie said warily as she sat in the empty chair.

"I'm John Perkins, Special Deputy Director at the Justice Department. I report to the attorney general and to the president. Only to them. As of today, you all report to me. Only to me." He was a stocky red-faced man with an old-fashioned flat top crowning his flushed face. His white sleeves were rolled up to his elbows, and a tie was loosely knotted at an open collar. His voice was deep and raspy—a smoker's voice.

Mackie didn't like his declaration of self-importance. Importance, she believed, should be earned not declared.

Perkins scanned the room. "I'll summarize why we're here and then make some introductions. You're here because someone out there is making gold." He crossed his arms and pressed his lips together. "Our job is to find him and stop him, and do it fast. Real fast. If word gets out that someone has figured out how to create gold, we'll have a worldwide financial catastrophe. The books in front of each of you describe some of the consequences." He reached down and picked up one of the books, turned to a marked page, and read aloud, "'Worldwide, only 165,000 tons of gold have been mined from the beginning of time. Put together, all that gold would make a cube twenty yards on a side.'" He looked up. "That's about the size of two big truck trailers. When you think that gold's been mined for thousands of years, not a very big pile. There's not a lot of gold out there." He went back to reading. "'It's hoarded by millions of people around the world and held as reserves by many governments. Many financial institutions also hold it as a reserve. If a new, possibly unlimited, supply of gold reaches the market, the price of gold will plummet. Two thousand dollars an ounce will become an historical aberration. One can only guess at the amount of decline, but it will be massive. The reason is that, although gold has a few commercial and jewelry uses, and some intrinsic value, its real value is based on its scarcity. If it's not scarce, it's just another metal.'"

Perkins paused and looked from face to face. "Its price could go down over ninety percent, folks. That's like a four-hundred-thousand-dollar house suddenly being worth less than thirty-five thousand. Your new car—a thousand bucks." He closed the book and leaned on the table with both hands. "That would be huge." Moving his eyes side to side around the room, he said, almost to himself, "Bigger than huge. People's wealth will simply evaporate. They'll become desperate.

"That's just a brief summary. What we have is someone who has sold a local hedge fund quite a bit of gold. The fund got suspicious and did some testing. It's gold, all right, but slightly different from the real thing. To be precise, pure twenty-four-karat mined gold weighs nineteen point three grams per cubic centimeter. It always has; it always will. This new stuff weighs only nineteen grams. The chemists say it's gold in all respects, but very, very slightly lighter. It passes all the tests for gold: nitric acid, electronic conductivity, even weight tests, unless they're taken to tenths of a gram. The weight discrepancy is less than one percent. They can't explain it. So our team has been pulled together with orders from the highest levels." He looked around the table. "Our job is to find out what's

21

going on and stop it."

"I'll now do those introductions." He pointed to each as he spoke. "John Ceshire here is the top I.T. guy at Justice. He can create, find, organize, or destroy any computer information out there."

Ceshire was young and wiry, with a round face and thick-lensed glasses. The man started to stand, but Perkins stopped him with a hand gesture.

"No need for any of you to say anything now. There'll be time to talk later." He gestured to his left. "Next to Ceshire here is Madeline Cartwright. Mrs. Cartwright is a financial historian from the Treasury Department. Her area of specialty is precious metals, and in particular, the most precious of them all—gold. She's here to teach us what we need to know about gold. She put together much of the book in front of you."

Cartwright was the older woman Mackie had noticed on her way in. Heavyset, with short brown hair, she raised a hand and smiled. As directed, she said nothing.

"Moving on, we have Douglas Meyer, on loan from NASA. Mr. Meyer is a chemist. He'll perform any necessary testing."

Meyer nodded his head. He was the oldest in the room. Wearing a white shirt and tie, he looked NASA.

"Ceshire, Cartwright, and Meyer are our inside team," Perkins said. "For the field, we have Agent Kathryn Mackie from Secret Service, who just joined us. She's been very active chasing and apprehending counterfeiters." Looking at Mackie, he said, "And I assume you caught a few today, Agent Mackie?"

"Yes, sir. It was a successful operation." She held his gaze until he blinked.

"Good." He pointed to a chair where a small, slightly rumpled man sat with hands clasped, eyes moving about the room. "Last but not least, another field agent on loan from our friends at Mossad, let me introduce—"

The man raised his hands, asking for silence, and spoke softly, "I am called Ishmael."

"Oh, a field name?" Perkins said. "Ishmael's from *Moby Dick*, isn't he?"

The man held Perkins' gaze. "Consider me a survivor in the real world, sir." He wore a short stubble of beard and shaggy black hair with a few gray patches. He returned his hands to their clasped position on the table.

"Yes, well…Ishmael is one of Mossad's longest-surviving and best field agents," said Perkins. "I expect him and Agent Mackie to make a good team."

"Sir," the man said, again raising his hands, this time shrugging in apology, "I have always worked alone." He grimaced in Mackie's direction with a small nod. "I do not work with partners."

All eyes turned to Mackie, who sat still with her hands folded on her book. She said nothing.

"This time I think you'll have to change your style, Ishmael." Perkins spoke in a soft but authoritative tone. "Your superiors knew this would be a team effort. They assured me of your dedication to carry out the mission."

"I have stayed alive all these years because I work only alone, sir. I don't see how I can change at this stage." His voice was soft but also firm.

There was silence as Perkins and the Israeli stared at each other.

Mackie raised her eyes to the Israeli. "Ishmael did not work alone."

"What do you mean?" he responded.

"He survived only because he had help. But for the coffin built by the carpenter on the *Pequod*, he would have drowned along with the others." She stared at and spoke only to him.

He pursed his lips and tented his fingers. "You do know your literature, Agent Mackie."

Papers were shuffled around the table, and a few muffled coughs broke the silence. The two agents continued to stare at each other.

Ishmael spoke first. "In deference to my superiors and my orders, why don't the two of us at least talk?" He looked over to Perkins, who still stood. "Is there a private room, sir?"

"Right there." Perkins pointed to a door at the other end of the room. "Small conference room on the other side."

Ishmael walked to the door and opened it, gesturing for Mackie to precede him. Inside was a small table. They sat on opposite sides, facing each other.

"First, Agent Mackie, your being a woman does not bother me in the least. Some of our best agents are women. My concern: what have you done as an agent?" He looked her in the eyes and pursed his lips. "Have you ever fought a man to the death?"

"I have fought men and women—never to the death—but always to victory." She leaned over the table till their faces were only a foot apart.

"What martial arts?"

"We train with the Marine Corps program. I hold a green belt."

"What weapons?"

"My personal preference in a pistol is the Glock. For a long gun, I use an MP5 submachine gun."

"Can you throw a knife?" He placed on the table a bone-handled carbon-fiber blade, which he pulled from an ankle holster. "A knife like this?"

Mackie thrust out her right hand, picked up the knife, and with a flick of her wrist, hurled it inches from his ear into the wall behind.

He didn't flinch. He raised his eyes to hers, stroking his chin. "Yes, you know knives." He held her gaze. "Can you kill a man or a woman?"

"Yes."

He sighed, straightened, and opened his arms. "And could you sleep with an enemy to get an advantage?"

She smiled a tight smile with lips pressed together. "No, I will not sleep with an enemy." She paused. "But…after I'm finished with him, he'll wish he'd been fucked." Raising her eyes and pointing at him, she said, "How about you, Ishmael? Will you fuck a woman for the mission?"

He stood and pointed a finger at her. "Agent Mackie, I would fuck a woman—or a man—if the mission required. I will kill or maim as necessary. I have no compunction, no conscience, no concerns beyond the mission."

She stood. "You are a hard man, sir."

"I come from a hard place. I have survived by being hard."

Mackie extended her hand across the table. "We now know a little of each other. Can we work together?"

He looked at her for a long moment. "We will try." He extended his hand to grasp hers before turning to open the door, muttering softly, "We will try." He pulled the knife from the wall and replaced it in his ankle holder. They walked back into the larger room.

All heads turned as they reentered the room.

"We worked out a few things," announced the Israeli. "We will be part of the team."

"Good," said Perkins. "Now back to business. You've seen the Top Secret stamps. Don't take that lightly." He walked to one end of the table and pulled down a large map of the world. "It's as important to keep the lid on this as it is to catch this guy." He pointed to the map. "Look at the highlighted countries. India, China, Russia, the Middle East, just for starters. Their people hold much of the world's consumer gold. But those and all these other countries—including us—have large amounts of gold in their vaults as liquid reserves for their currency. No one is technically on the gold standard anymore, but it's still a very important government asset around the world. If word gets out that someone's making gold, there will be panic. Could lead to a worldwide economic implosion."

He nodded grimly. "And you know what that means? That means war, folks. Someone will attack someone else. India will move on Pakistan, or China on one of its neighbors, or some dictator who's lost his gold riches will act out of desperation. Our job is to stop that from happening."

Mackie had sat and started to skim the booklet. She looked up and raised her hand. "Sir, one question?"

"Sure, Mackie, what is it?"

"What's the crime, sir?"

All heads turned to her.

"What the hell do you mean, what's the crime?" he barked. "This guy's counterfeiting gold!"

"Looks like he, or she, is making gold, sir, but counterfeiting usually deals with official currencies. As you just said, gold isn't anyone's official currency."

Perkins glared at her with pursed lips. "Look, Mackie, don't you worry about the crime. Your job is to find the guy. We'll stop him, and others can figure out the crime. You have any problem with that?"

"I have no problem, Mr. Perkins. I just wonder if the guy's really breaking any law. We'll find him, but someone has to figure out what to do next."

"We'll do that, Mackie. I promise you, we'll do that. First, though, let's get down to business and figure out who has this Midas touch."

That evening, Ishmael—his real name was Michael Bent—sent a coded email to his superiors. He was from a small group within Mossad known as Metsada. His specialty was killing.

He typed with two fingers:

> *The group has been assembled. As expected, my attempt to work alone was resisted. I am partnered with Special Agent Kathryn Mackie of the counterfeiting office of their Secret Service. She is competent. I should be able to work with her until the source is located. I will then have to decide what to do with her.*

⟡

The same evening, Mackie called her boyfriend, Jonathon Cook, an attorney in a large Washington law firm. She was more nervous than she had been that morning confronting the counterfeiters.

"Jonathon, it's me.... Well, that's why I'm calling. About next week. I have a problem.... I know everything's booked and scheduled. I know. It's just... Oh, shit, Jonathon! I've been called onto some big emergency task force. I know they won't let me leave.... Our vacation is important to me. It's all I've been thinking about. But they won't let me go.... I know this is America, and I'm no one's slave. But they can fire me, and this is so secret, they'd probably detain me if I tried to leave. Look, you go, and I'll try to fly down for at least a couple of days.... I know it would be different. I just don't know what to say.... Honey, there's a slim chance something's going to break soon, but I don't think so. We've been assigned to a little Hitler called John Perkins from the Department of Justice. I can't even tell you what we're doing."

She was quiet for a second. "But, Jonathon, there's maybe one thing you could do which might speed things up. A little legal research. Please? Pretty please? I'll pay you back, I promise. I'd like to know if someone has committed a crime if he finds a way to make..." She paused, trying to decide what she could say. "To make copper.... Yeah, just like that. Some mad scientist finds a way to boil lead and turn it into copper. Is that illegal?... Thanks, Jonathon. I'll call over the weekend. We'll get through this." She choked back a sob. "I'm so sorry."

After disconnecting, Mackie went back to her top-secret gold book. She was still surprised to read how serious the consequences would be if gold were devalued.

Roughly half the world's gold is held as jewelry, with the other half in bullion or coin. If someone can make gold rather than mine it, there is no limit to how much can be made. One ton a day in one facility, a half ton in another, and the supply of gold could double in ten years. The marketplace would not wait for that to happen.

A sudden drop in gold's market value would cause chaos in the world's financial markets. As its value rose toward two thousand dollars an ounce, gold became widely accepted by financial institutions as collateral for loans, stock purchases, and international letters of credit. If its value plummets, more collateral would be demanded, leading to the forced sale of other assets, and, eventually, fire sales of gold itself. Next, calls would be made on the credit default swaps that insure the loans. It would create a snowball effect similar to what happened in 2008. In 2008, governments limited the pain by guaranteeing some of the defaulting financial obligations. No country, however, can guaranty the value of a metal that can be made as easily as pouring glass. At 160,000 tons, the world's gold supply is worth over $100 trillion. Much of that value would disappear overnight.

She fell asleep with the book in her hands.

CHAPTER 4

THE DELIVERY MAN

"Three fucking ounces!" Tom Gleason muttered as he walked back to his car. "Who cares about three fucking ounces?" Overweight, huffing as much from frustration as exhaustion, the old man threw the metal case onto the passenger seat and slid backward behind the steering wheel before swiveling his feet to the pedals. Now empty and light, the case bounced against the door and onto the floor. "Shit. All I need now is for the goddamned dye package to explode." He looked over at the silver briefcase he had delivered from Bonita. Two combination dials projected from the clasps, and metal strapping circled under the handle into another lock. He held his breath and lifted it gently to the seat. He'd now have to report this three-ounce discrepancy. Since the case had weighed a good twenty pounds, he couldn't understand the big deal over a few ounces.

The suited man at the hedge fund had returned the case to him after about thirty minutes, a frown on his face. "Mr. Gleason, we have found a shortage. A three-ounce shortage. This is a serious matter."

"Hey, mister, I'm only the delivery man. I brought it over from this guy, David, just as he gave it to me. You'll have to talk to him."

"I wish we could, Mr. Gleason, but your company's our only contact. Tell Mr. David that we'll have to talk to him before taking any more deliveries. And tell him we've adjusted his payment appropriately."

"I'll tell him. I'm meeting him at five over in Bonita. I'll ask him to call you."

He looked at the case and breathed a sigh of relief. At least it hadn't exploded on him. Turning the ignition key with his right hand to get the air conditioning, with his left he pulled out his phone to text his delivery confirmation. *Pain-in-the-ass rules with these deliveries,* he thought. *What the hell am I delivering that called for all this rigmarole?*

Cnfm dlvy, he texted. He started to put the phone back in his pocket, shook his head, and added, Clm a 3 oz shortage.

He wasn't out of the parking lot before the phone rang.

"Yeah. Tom here."

The voice that responded was anxious. "Tom, what'd you mean, a three-ounce *shortage?*"

"I don't know, sir. They took the case from me and brought it back after a while saying something about a three-ounce shortage. It's a hell of a lot lighter now, so I guess they took out whatever was in it."

"Did you open it?"

He listened and frowned. "Of course I didn't open it. It's locked up like Fort Knox. And the guy claims it's also protected by some type of exploding dye package. What the hell am I delivering, anyway?"

"Tom, you just make the deliveries. Don't need to ask questions."

"Fine. Okay. No more questions. But these guys say no more deliveries till they talk to Mr. David about the claimed shortages. I'm supposed to tell him that when I return the case. That okay with you?"

"Yeah, sure, tell him what they need."

"Okay, I'm seeing him at five to return the briefcase. I'll tell him."

Gleason was parked in the far corner of the Home Depot parking lot in Bonita Springs when Mr. David pulled next to him and beckoned the delivery man to join him in his car. Gleason didn't like being summoned with a curling index finger, but he lifted the case carefully, got out of his car, and walked over to the other vehicle, a black Lexus, and slid into the passenger seat.

"Little bit of a problem, sir."

"What do you mean?"

"They told me there was a shortage. Whatever the hell that means. They said they had to talk to you—"

"What do you mean, shortage?" Mr. David spit out, hands still on his steering wheel and staring straight ahead. "What the hell happened?"

"I only know what they told me, Mr. David. The man said there was a three-ounce shortage, that they needed to talk to you before taking any more deliveries. He also said they had adjusted your payment."

Mr. David's head snapped around, and he stared at the man. "Let's see the case." He took it and leaned it against the wheel, bending to look at the locks. "Looks okay," he said, nodding. "No sign of tampering."

"Look, Mr. David, it was never out of my possession except when they had it. They obviously opened it and took something out, 'cause it's a lot lighter now." He shrugged. "I don't know what's going on. Guess you'll have to talk to them."

Mr. David sat for a moment with his hands on the briefcase and stared straight ahead. He finally pressed his lips together and gave a quick nod.

"You're right, Mr. Gleason." He pulled an envelope out of his pocket and handed it to the man. "Here's your payment. I'll take care of everything. Don't worry about it. But remember"—the finger was straight now and pointing—"there is to be no talk about these deliveries. They are to remain confidential. Tell Mr. Acme that I'll call if I need another."

Gleason took the envelope and got out of the car, thinking, *Didn't say when he needs another delivery. Said "if." There won't be any more. Something is wrong.*

He stood as the Lexus squealed away, and he saw a grim look on the face of the driver. "The guy's pissed," he whispered. "He's really pissed."

CHAPTER 5
THE HEDGE FUND

After discussion, the team agreed the first step was to get to the hedge fund which had reported the problem with its gold: Gold Coast Investments in Boca Raton, an hour north of Miami.

"They brought a gold bar into the FBI and said it was suspicious," explained Perkins. "Said it tested positive as pure gold but that it was too big. Came from a supplier on the west coast who bought and melted old jewelry." He shrugged. "Guess that's a big business nowadays. All the old folks selling their jewelry and gold coins. The hedge fund reported that it weighed a kilo as stamped, but seemed a little bit bigger than their other kilo bars. The FBI lab tested it and agreed it was pure gold—the real stuff—twenty-four karat. But it did measure slightly larger than normal. No one gave it too much attention till they brought in the second bar a few days ago." He was seated at the table and pulled a briefcase from the floor, put it on the table, and popped it open.

"Here's the second bar." He lifted a yellow ingot from the case and placed it gingerly in the middle of the table. "Same problem. A little too big. Taller than it should be. The lab guys concluded that a bad jewelry melt couldn't have happened twice, only a month apart. So they did their own melt and measured a known quantity, a cubic centimeter." He pulled a black gem box from the briefcase and opened it on the table. Inside, a small, golden cube glistened. All four bent over the table to view it as Perkins continued.

"There it is. A cubic centimeter of pure gold." He picked it up in his right hand and jiggled it. "But it's too light, folks; weighs only nineteen grams." He put it back on the table and tapped it with his finger. "As I said, every piece of gold, from ancient times till today, has weighed nineteen point three grams per cubic centimeter." He put both pieces back in the case and snapped it shut.

"Mackie and"—he paused with a grimace—"Ishmael, get to the hedge fund first thing in the morning and find out who supplied this stuff. He's not just melting bad gold earrings." He stood to leave, adding, "He's messing with history."

Mackie and the Israeli met at eight the following morning to drive north. The pool had given her a Taurus; at least it was not a compact. She had finished reading Cartwright's report that morning.

"Learned a lot more about gold than a girl needs to know," she said with a smile as she drove. "Did you know that most personally owned gold is in China and India? They hoard the stuff. Like cash in a mattress."

"One big difference, though," the Israeli responded. "Cash loses value in that mattress. Gold, on the other hand, has tripled in value. At today's prices, it's the most valuable thing those hoarders own."

"Yeah, you're right. Wish I had bought some gold. Maybe some of those Jerusalem gold coins I read about last night. I see that Israel just started issuing them."

He turned slowly and gazed at Mackie for a moment before turning back straight in his seat. "They're called Jerusalem of Gold, not Jerusalem

Gold. Jerusalem has no gold. But we believe Jerusalem is gold." He waved a hand. "But I'm splitting hairs. Yes, we now make and issue our own gold coins. One ounce. Sell for a bit more than two thousand each with a collector's premium. Don't know where they get the gold—probably Africa. I'll see about getting you one after the mission, because we're also protecting Israel's gold coins." He nodded to himself. "We're protecting Jerusalem."

She smiled. "That would be nice. But I'll pay for it."

"I imagine you will, Agent Mackie. Now let's figure out what we're going to say to these guys. Remember, we can't let them think someone's making gold."

Gold Coast Investments was one of a growing number of hedge funds based in south Florida. Agent Mackie had read its profile the evening before. About a billion in assets under management, and it was one of a growing number of hedge funds that held actual gold bullion as an investment and as a hedge. The company occupied the fifth floor of a midrise office building off the Sawgrass Expressway. Mackie and her partner were ushered into a conference room and told that Mr. Stoddard would be there in a minute. The Israeli had been convinced that the name Ishmael wouldn't cut it for field work, so he told them his real name was Michael Bent. Maybe it was. They were issued identification cards as special agents with the Department of Justice.

Mackie looked professional in slacks, a white knit top, and black flats. Bent was in black, all the way down to his Adidas running shoes. The conference room overlooked a sculpted golf course speckled with white sand traps. They walked to the expansive window and looked out.

"Ever played golf, Kate?"

"Only the miniature courses as a kid," she answered as she gazed down. "Never had the inclination—or the time or money—as a kid. More into hoops and stickball or whatever else was happening on the street." She sighed. "Guess I always viewed it as a rich white man's sport."

"Tiger isn't white," he replied.

"Oh, you'd be surprised, Michael. Scratch his skin, and you'll find the whitest white man around." She turned to him and asked, "How about you? You a golfer?"

He pointed below and tapped the window. "Not enough land in Israel for many courses like that. But I learned to play once, for a mission. Had to do a little golfing in South Africa. Pretending to be on vacation to set up an execution."

"Execution?" She leaned back with raised eyebrows.

"Yeah. Guy had retired from the PLO after shooting a bunch of missiles at us. Tried to disappear in Cape Town. I found him. He was a golfer. So I learned golf."

"And…?"

"Killed him on the turn. The ninth green. Right in front of the clubhouse." His hands were clasped behind his back as he remembered that time. "The guy bent to get his ball out of the cup, and the cup exploded in his face." He nodded. "Just about took his head off."

"Making a statement?"

He sighed. "Oh, yeah, we were making a statement. Letting them know there's nowhere to hide. You hurt us, we'll find you and hurt you."

"So you're the judge, jury, and executioner?"

"You could put it that way." He turned from the window and faced Mackie. "I've killed fourteen people in twenty years. I think your drones kill a thousand every year. I don't see a difference, other than we send a man and you use a machine. Same result…"

A discreet knock on the door announced the arrival of Mr. Stoddard.

Stoddard wore a dark blue suit with light blue shirt, checked tie, and handkerchief peaking above his breast pocket. A scent of expensive cologne accompanied him as he entered and closed the door. He carried his hands clasped at belt level before extending his right arm to shake hands, first with Mackie and then with the Israeli.

"Herb Stoddard. I'm the office administrator here at Gold Coast. Ms....?"

"Mackie, Kate Mackie, and this is Michael Bent."

"You're from the FBI?"

"No, we're actually with the Department of Justice." She extended her card. "The Justice Department has a special division that deals with special metals like gold, silver, platinum. You name it, we cover it. Usually we're dealing with theft, but every once in a while, questions come up about whether a precious metal is really precious, whether it's genuine. So we were called in by the FBI to look into this gold you acquired." She thought the cover story sounded okay, simple and not far from the truth.

"Fine," replied Stoddard, gesturing for them to take seats as he sat. "I assume you've seen the bars we left with the FBI?"

"Yes, sir," Mackie continued to take the lead, as they had agreed in the car. "We've tested them quite thoroughly."

"Well, is it real gold?" Stoddard asked, leaning forward with his hands on the table. Droplets of sweat glistened on his forehead. "Am I okay, or am I in trouble here?"

"Let's just say it's more or less the real thing," she answered. "We'll get into that. First, though, we need to know about your supplier, where it came from."

"I'm embarrassed to say we don't know a lot about him. His name is Henry David. From the west coast, the Naples area. Approached us a couple of months ago about selling us gold bullion he was acquiring from a consortium of jewelry stores and collectors. With the price of gold going through the stratosphere, everyone's selling their old coins and jewelry, and there's quite a market in it after it's recycled into bars and ingots."

"Why did your firm need gold, Mr. Stoddard?" asked Bent as he entered the conversation.

"Everyone needs gold nowadays." Stoddard opened his hands in a gesture of obviousness. "Some funds are pure gold funds. Some, and we're one of these, hedge their other investments with gold. The banking houses are even now accepting gold as collateral for loans."

"But why this Mr. David?" Mackie's partner continued. "Why not an established gold bullion supplier, like a PMF or APMEX?"

She saw the beads of sweat grow on Stoddard's forehead, and his fingers were clasping and unclasping on the table.

"Guess it wasn't one of our—no, I guess my—finest hours." His eyes were downcast on the table and no longer directed at the two agents. "Usually you pay the current spot price plus a five-percent commission to the seller." He shook his head. "Mr. David made a very attractive offer. He said his group had been collecting gold for a number of months at much lower prices. So he was willing to sell at the spot without any commission. That was a huge savings. Five percent direct to our bottom line. I was a bit of a hero around here." He sighed. "At least for a while."

"You must have checked him out," said the Israeli.

"A little bit, but not in depth. He had a website and a bunch of reference letters. Looked very legitimate." He straightened in his chair and shook a finger at them. "We checked out the gold, though. Real carefully. Brought in a chemist from the University of Miami, who did a bunch of assay tests on a sample. She gave it her blessing, said it was the real thing. Pure, twenty-four-karat gold."

"What caused you to bring that first bar to the FBI, Mr. Stoddard?" asked Mackie. "After all your tests…did you test each bar you bought?"

"Definitely," he answered in a firm voice. "Every goddamned bar was tested. I used due diligence. No matter what *they* say." He pointed his thumb over his shoulder to the offices behind.

"So…?"

"They were too big!" he exclaimed. "When the first shipment of ten bars was put into our safe, they stacked a little higher than the bars already stored there. Each bar was slightly taller than the old ones. Not a lot. Just one millimeter. But when you stack them ten on top of each other, that's a ten millimeter difference between the two stacks. Suddenly very noticeable. They each weighed a kilo, and they each tested pure. But they were too goddamned tall!" he shouted and threw his hands up. "Too goddamned tall."

He paused and took a deep breath. "Please, tell me what's going on. What did you mean, *more or less* the real thing? I need to know. My job's at stake." He sat looking back and forth at the two agents. "I'm sorry. I'll be fine. Just a little bit of pressure around here."

"I think I can give you some reassurances, Mr. Stoddard," Kate said, starting the cover story. "What you bought was mostly gold, but not a hundred percent. We think your supplier has come up with a way to blend lesser-karat gold with twenty-four, resulting in a bar that has a core with some impurities. Since almost all testing is done on the outside surface, it tests pure. Only by melting down the entire bar or drilling out a core sample can you discover the problem."

"And you're right, sir," added Michael. "They weigh a kilo, but because of the impurities, they're slightly bigger than the real thing."

"But are they worth anything?" whispered the shaken man. "We're talking about almost a million dollars we paid this guy. What're they worth?"

"They certainly have value, Mr. Stoddard," replied Mackie. "We really don't know how much. But there is a lot of gold in those bars." She tapped her hand on the table. "But we have to get back to finding this Henry David or whatever his real name is. My guess is that most of the background info he gave you was fake. How were the bars delivered?"

"That's it!" Stoddard perked up. "The delivery service. I have receipts, and I can describe the guy who made both deliveries. Old, fat guy. Couldn't have been smart enough to do this himself."

CHAPTER 6
A SOLAR LOBSTER BAKE

How the hell could there be a shortage? Conan's mind raced as he sped north on I-75 to get to his riverside lab and try to figure things out. *I have the best damn scale available, and I know the bars weigh a kilo. All the tests reflect twenty-four-karat purity. So how can there be a shortage? I'll be up all night on this, and tomorrow's my damn solar lobster bake. A couple dozen students in my backyard for lobsters and corn cooked in solar-heated water.*

He stamped down on the gas pedal. "Shit, shit, shit!" he yelled. *There's just no way.*

He reached over and fumbled with the lock tumblers to open the case. He wasn't worried about any dye package; that was just a story he made up to make the delivery guy more careful. The car swerved onto the grooved rumble strip on the side of the road. A horn blared at him, but he managed to pop the top and pull out the envelope. Grabbing the flap with his teeth, he ripped it open and pulled out the check. He cursed again. It was forty-six hundred dollars short, just about one percent. *So they're claiming a one-percent shortage. Great. Where the hell do I find one percent?*

41

◦❧◦

"Professor Conan, what an amazing setting," gushed one of the students the next afternoon as they stood on his back deck overlooking the Caloosahatchee River. Twenty had arrived for his annual cookout. They were enrolled in the two small seminars he taught on alternative energy sources. He was mixing and talking with the group, exhausted after the night's futile efforts to uncover any flaw in his processes. He had found none. Now he had to put on a dog-and-pony show for these kids.

If you only knew how amazing, he thought, walking over to the table that held three large stainless steel pots. He faced the group. "Remember our discussions about heating with sunlight? This afternoon, a practical demonstration. Grab a beer or soft drink, and I'll explain how we're going to cook with the heat of the sun. We'll regroup here in an hour. If you go across the road to the marsh"—he pointed across the street—"stay on the dirt road. It goes for miles, and there's a lot of wildlife out there. You don't want to step on those critters."

He watched as most of the students scattered, grabbing drinks. One, a girl—actually an attractive grown woman—strolled to the towers and then to his canal with the filtration system. She appeared to be talking on her cell phone. He noticed she never put it away, holding it at her waist when not talking. Was she taking pictures?

Later, the students gathered, and he began his explanation.

"As we all know, water boils at two hundred twelve degrees. Does anyone remember the amount of heat that can be achieved with sunlight?"

"I think you told us six thousand degrees," answered an attractive female student who stood alone near the front of the group. Her dark skin and black hair pointed to Latino heritage. He'd noticed her in the classroom sessions. She was the one with the phone.

"Right…Linda, I believe?"

"Yes, Professor." She smiled, showing very nice white teeth.

"Look over in my side yard." He pointed to his left. "You'll see three towers. Each has a special parabolic mirror mounted on the top to capture and focus the sun's rays. I have to be able to move the mirrors to different angles since the Earth is always moving, so I devised a remote positioning device." He picked up what looked like a television remote and pointed it at one of the towers. "Can you see the mirror move? I'm making it circle clockwise, left to right. Here, who wants to give it a try?"

Linda stepped forward.

He handed her the device. "Now let me guide your finger here over the scrolling wheel. Watch the mirror move in the same direction as your finger. There, you have it. Can you see the ray of sunlight moving around on the ground?"

"Yes, I see it. That's neat."

After several others had used it, Conan addressed them again. "For today, I've calculated and preset the mirrors to focus sufficient sun on these three pots to bring two gallons of water to a boil in fifteen minutes. That will be much less than six thousand degrees. Closer to a thousand. Maybe you could help by bringing two gallons of water to each pot." He glanced at his watch. "The mirrors will turn and automatically focus at two o'clock, ten minutes from now. So let's get the water in the pots. We want each pot to have exactly two gallons. Take the water from that pipe that's draining into the trough. It's filtered water, fully drinkable."

The water was poured into the pots. The students all looked at their watches and the towers, their heads moving back and forth like spectators at a tennis match.

"Professor, that middle pot seems to have more water in it," one student said. "You said everything had to be precise."

Conan walked over and looked at the pots. "No, it's fine. The middle pot's a bit narrower than the others, so the water reaches a slightly higher—" He stopped in mid sentence. I'll be damned, he thought. *That might just be it. Same volume, different height. What about same weight, different height? Gotta get these kids out of here to figure this out!*

"Professor, it's two o'clock. The mirrors are moving!"

He broke out of his reverie and stumbled through the next two hours, his thoughts elsewhere.

⁓

Conan jerked awake. His head lay on his arms on the computer keyboard. He remembered coming in as soon as the first students started to leave, saying he had a conference call. After making some calculations, he thought he had figured out the problem, but his exhaustion caught up with him, and he fell asleep at his desk. Looking over to a clock, he saw it was six. He must have slept for more than an hour. He heard some noises from the kitchen and went to investigate.

"Linda, what are you doing?"

She looked up from the sink and smiled. "I couldn't leave this mess for you. I saw you asleep in there, so I figured I'd get some of it cleaned up. It was a wonderful afternoon. The least I could do."

He shook out the grogginess. "Well, thanks. Thanks a lot, Linda. Not at all necessary. Are you the only one left?"

"Yep. Just the two of us, Professor. I'm pretty much done. Any chance of offering a poor girl one of those cold beers?"

He hesitated for a moment. "Of course. And I think I'll join you. Before I fell asleep, I think I figured out a problem I've been having with one of my experiments. So yeah, let's have a beer and celebrate."

"I love celebrations, Professor."

⁓

A couple of beers led to a couple of glasses of wine. Before long, they were seated on his deck, watching the sun set on the western horizon.

"There's a lot of power in the sun," he said, looking over to Linda, who was now curled in a chair with her legs tucked under. His gaze lingered on her long, tawny legs and a blouse open enough to show a peek of her breasts. And she had those beautiful white teeth. He smiled. "The sun's power never stops. We simply lose sight of it at night. Let's toast the setting sun and the power that will return at dawn and again and again every morning."

"Sounds good to me." Raising her glass, she said, "To the sun." Turning back to him, she added, "But you haven't told me what we're celebrating. What did you figure out?"

He smiled and took a sip of wine. "Let's put it this way: If I were to give you something that was bigger than it should be, would you call it a shortage?"

She shrugged and set her wine glass on the table, thinking. "Probably not a shortage. Wouldn't it really be an overage?"

"That's exactly what I figured out!" He stood and looked toward where the sun had been a moment ago. Just a glow remained on the horizon. "I figured that a shortage can sometimes really be an overage." He looked down at her. "And after those profound words, we have to figure out what to do with you."

Her eyebrows rose and she gave him a small smile. "What do you have in mind, Professor?"

"Well, neither one of us should be driving, so unless I can get you a cab, you might be here for the night."

"There's no one waiting up for me. I can do as I wish."

"What do you wish, Linda?"

"I think I'll spend the night here. Maybe a little more wine, a little more celebrating."

⁓

Conan had never forgotten the Boston episode, but he was only slightly troubled by bedding a student. His female companionship over the years had been short relationships and one-night stands, usually with older women, but Linda was not a kid. He thought she was probably a lot closer to his age than that of most students. And she showed she had experience. They remained on the porch, drinking wine, till full darkness enveloped them. She then joined him on his lap, bent close, and kissed him.

"I've never been with a professor," she whispered in his ear. She tongued his ear and caressed his groin. "But I think I'm going to like it. Let's go inside and find out. I'll bring the wine."

Once inside, she pulled him to the bed, "Let me be the teacher tonight, Professor. I'm going to be on top. It's much more fun." She straddled him. "You just lie still. I'll do all the work."

After sex, Conan fell asleep. Linda rolled off his body and lay still, listening to his breathing. She knew she had about two hours before the drug would wear off. She lifted the sheet very slowly, slipped out of bed, and went exploring.

CHAPTER 7
FINDING GLEASON

It didn't take the two agents long to locate the delivery service. The receipt named Bonita Bees Deliveries, and although the name of the driver was illegible, they had his description.

"I'll call right now," Mackie said as they sat alone in the conference room after Stoddard went to get the remaining eighteen bars. They wanted to test them all. She started to dial the number obtained from information.

The Israeli held up his hand. "Wait a moment, Kate. The place is in Naples, less than two hours away. I've found face-to-face is often better than by phone." He leaned over the table with hands grasping the edge. "Let's just drive over there and hit him cold. We don't know if he's involved or a dupe."

She put the phone away. "You're right. We'll surprise him."

Just then Stoddard came back wheeling a large black case on its built-in rollers. "Here they are. Eighteen of them."

"Thanks, Mr. Stoddard," said Mackie as she stood. "Slight change of plans. We're going to drive to Naples to see this delivery service. Don't really want to be carrying forty pounds of gold in the trunk. So we're calling our office in Miami to have the bars picked up. They'll probably use some sort of van or armored car. That okay with you?"

"Sure. It's fine. I'll just roll it back to the safe."

As he turned to leave, Michael stopped him. "Mr. Stoddard?"

Stoddard turned.

"This is all very confidential, sir. We don't want anyone to get word of this investigation."

"Folks, I can assure you that no one here is going to say anything to anyone. We're very embarrassed. We manage people's money and promise to exercise the highest level of skill and fidelity. We don't want this to get out. We want it fixed—as quickly and quietly as possible."

"Good," Bent answered. "We're on the same page."

The drive to Naples on I-75—Alligator Alley—was uneventful. It was Mackie's first time crossing the Everglades on the divided highway. "A hell of a lot of grass," she observed. "Yeah," her companion muttered, "someone called it a sea of grass. Look at the grassy waves caused by the wind."

The delivery company in Naples was on Fifth Avenue, but on the east side of Route 41, not in the high-rent district. The manager, Mr. Acme, was cooperative.

"Sure, I remember that customer. A bit odd. Almost a mystery man. I think we did six deliveries for him to the east coast. Hedge funds, I think. He always met my driver at the Home Depot parking lot, gave him a case and an address, and picked up the case from him at the end of the same day."

"How about a name and address, sir?" asked Mackie.

"Let me look here." Acme pulled open a file drawer. "Haven't heard from the guy in a couple of weeks. I remember my driver said there was some problem with the last delivery." He shuffled through the papers. "I don't think we did anything wrong." He pulled out a paper with a flourish. "Here it is. I have it in the 'Miami' file since we don't do that many deliveries to the east coast. Yeah, six deliveries in the Boca area. Not really Miami."

"Name and address?" she asked again, impatiently.

Acme looked up. "Name's easy. It's Mr. Henry David. But I don't see any address. He always paid the driver. Charged him four hundred fifty each time."

"What about a phone number, Mr. Acme? You must have been able to contact him," persisted the agent.

"You know, that was funny. I remember him saying something about traveling a lot and being hard to reach." He leaned back in his chair and nodded. "He always called me. I guess I never really had a way of reaching the guy." He sat straight and looked at the agents. "So what's this guy done? Am I in trouble? What were we delivering?"

"No, sir, you're not in trouble," Mackie answered. "But we have to find Mr. David. How about your driver?"

"That's Gleason. Not a bad guy. Never missed a pickup. I think he lives in Bonita. Want me to call him?"

"No, not right now," Bent leaned forward and gestured toward the paper in Acme's hand. "Why don't you give us his address? We'll drive over to his place."

"Sure. Whatever you want." He wrote an address on a slip of paper.

Reading the address, Mackie stood to leave, but Bent stayed seated and stared hard at Acme. "Don't call Gleason. We want to talk to him without any alert from you. Okay?"

"Sure. Whatever."

"Oh, Mr. Acme," Bent said, "how did he pay you?"

"Well, it wasn't cash, if that's what you're suggesting, sir." He looked again at the paper he had been studying earlier. "Looks like he used money orders," he muttered as he looked at a ledger sheet. "I guess that's as good as cash. But it's not cash. And it was all reported."

"Mr. Acme, we're not the IRS," added Mackie as she grabbed Bent's arm to urge him to back off. "All we want to do is locate Mr. David. We probably will need copies of all your paperwork on this guy, but right now we're going to see Mr. Gleason. Someone will get back to you about the documents." Raising her palms in reassurance, she added, "Don't worry. You're not in any trouble. You've been a big help."

Gleason was eager to help when they met him at his condominium. He remembered Henry David and didn't seem surprised that the law wanted to find him. But he couldn't add anything to what Acme had already told the agents except for the car; he remembered David's car.

"A black Lexus 460, the big one. Don't see many of those around." He ran a hand across his thinning hair. "The last time, when I sat in it and took a little shit from him, I remember it smelled new." He pointed in the air, saying, "You find that car, you find Henry David. And you know what?" He looked back and forth at the two agents. "I bet that's not his name. I bet the son of a bitch is no more Henry David than I'm Jackie Gleason."

CHAPTER 8

THE MORNING AFTER

Conan woke with sticky eyes, sandpaper for a tongue, and a throbbing head. He was alone in the bed, but he heard light clattering in the kitchen. And he remembered his guest of the evening. *What a night.* But he didn't think he had drunk that much. He moved slowly into the bathroom to clean up.

"Hey, Sleepyhead," he heard as he brushed his teeth. "You finally awake?"

"Be out in a minute," he gurgled.

She was on the bed when he came out. Naked and smiling with those beautiful white teeth.

"Coffee's on. But I thought we could start breakfast here," she said. "If you're up for it…Oh, looks like you're getting up for it. Why don't you be the teacher this morning? I'm awfully hungry. Here, let me help you get all the way up."

Afterward, Linda said she had to leave to meet a group that needed her car.

"I'll see you at class on Tuesday," she whispered as she slipped out of bed. "Thanks for the party…and the breakfast."

❧

Conan stayed in bed for a few moments and heard Linda leave and drive away. Other than Marge, the older bartender from PJ's Lounge whom he had befriended on the way home a few months ago, this was the only encounter he'd had with a woman in more than a year. He couldn't figure out how it had all come about. No way she was just pushing for a grade. She had been much too intense for that. She certainly knew how to please a guy.

But why was he still groggy?

As she had said, the coffee was on. He poured a cup and began to remember his excitement from the night before when he realized what might be wrong with the weight and size of the gold bars. He walked into his office, surprised to find the door ajar. Then, bending to his computer, he was surprised again to find it turned off. He didn't think he had shut it down the night before when he woke from his nap on the keyboard. *Why do I feel someone's been in here?* he thought. He shuffled to the printer and pulled it away from the wall to look at the meter on the back. Someone had made a lot of copies. At nine o'clock he made the call. He had to be insistent about talking directly to the doctor.

"Dr. Guzzner, this is Professor Henry Conan. Haven't seen you in a few months, but I need some real quick assistance…. No, the emergency room isn't what I need. I ran into a problem in a bar last night, and I think…I think someone might have slipped me a mickey…. I know, I know. I'm not asking you for anything other than a blood test. I've drawn some blood before it can dissipate. I need the blood tested for Rohypnol, GHB, or whatever else is like a date-rape drug…. No, I wasn't raped." *Actually, I guess I was,* he thought. "But I might have been knocked out for a while…. Dr. Guzzner, if I was asleep, I wouldn't exactly remember it. All I need is for you to have the blood tested. I can drop the vial by your office…. I know insurance won't cover it. I'll pay for the test….

Good, thanks. I'll be by in about an hour."

He sat back, sure he was being paranoid, but someone had been in his office, on his computer, making copies. Maybe Linda had been too good to be true.

CHAPTER 9
A TEAM MEETING

"These Lexus dealers have been a pain in the ass," announced Perkins to the assembled group on Tuesday morning. "First, their businesspeople weren't in over the weekend. Then they had to check with corporate. Now they say they want a subpoena or a court order. The new privacy laws, they claim."

"Thought those only applied to doctors," Mackie said.

"You might be right," Perkins grumbled, "but our hands are tied because we can't explain why we want to know everyone in south Florida who owns a black Lexus 460. So we're going to find a judge, make up a story, and get a damn subpoena. But it's going to be a couple more days before we get the names."

"What about the other deliveries?" Michael Bent asked. "Gold Coast said they only got two."

"Better news there. That guy Acme didn't insist on a subpoena. We got his delivery papers. Two other hedge funds. All in the Boca area. Two deliveries each."

"We can talk to them," Mackie added. "See if they have any more information on this Henry David."

"I think we have to hold on that," said Perkins, looking apologetic. "This guy almost certainly used the same approach. They won't know shit about him. And then we have two more companies and who knows how many more people who know we're investigating this gold. We have to keep the lid on this."

"What about the name Henry David?" the Israeli asked.

John Ceshire, the computer specialist, jumped in. "Better luck there. I've come up with…" he looked at his notes. "One thousand thirteen hundred and seven possibilities—either H. David or Henry David. We've given the names and addresses to local police and the FBI for drive-bys looking for a black Lexus. Nothing yet."

Bent nodded. "Probably has to be done. But as Gleason said, that's probably not his name."

"Look," Perkins said, "the car's our best lead. It might take a few more days, but not much can happen in a couple of days. We'll have the list by Friday, and it sure as hell won't be thirteen hundred names."

CHAPTER 10
A HOUSE CLEANING

"Jesus Christ! She did drug me," he muttered as he hung up the phone. "She fucked me, drugged me, and then fucked me again."

He was standing at his workbench, recalling Dr. Guzzner's report: "You were right, Professor. There was GHB in your blood—a common date-rape type of drug. What's going on?"

Conan had thought quickly. He didn't want this taken any further. "Nothing to worry about, Doctor. Think I was in the wrong bar at the wrong time. Everything's fine. Just woke up feeling strange and wanted to check it out. I appreciate your help."

He was so mad, his temples throbbed and his hands clenched. He had to think. Twenty years of effort, and now this. What the hell was happening? Why was this…this Linda…looking at his stuff? He should have known she was too good to be true. But who was she, and who had sent her? Someone wanted to find out about his gold. But who was it and how would they know?

"Fine," he finally announced to the empty room. "I'll make this place squeaky clean. There'll be no gold here. It's all going on vacation. But I have to find out who the hell she is, why she was here. Oh, God, what do

I do then?" He clasped his hands to his face. "What do I do with her then?"

"Mr. Brown, I have a safe I need delivered to a storage unit.... No, tomorrow won't do. I need it picked up today.... Don't worry. I'll pay what it takes. I need a truck here this afternoon.... I'll have five hundred for them when they pick it up. I need it to go into one of your small, climate-controlled bins. I'm going to store some old books in it.... Fine. I can do cash. And let me know what a year's storage will cost. I'll pay for a year up front.... Three o'clock is fine. Here's my address. I'll be here."

CHAPTER 11
FLORIDA GULF COAST UNIVERSITY

The next day, Conan was glad to see that Linda Chavez was in class. He had worried she might disappear. He hadn't even known her last name, but that had been easy to get from the registrar's office. Her records were sparse. There was almost no information about her background. She was auditing two courses—his two courses. That was the extent of her studies. After class, he moved quickly to catch up with her outside the building.

"Linda, hope you're not running away."

She smiled. "Nothing of the kind, Professor. Just trying to get to my next class."

My ass, he thought. *There isn't any other class.* "Linda, I have something more important than any class."

"Professor, maybe we shouldn't, right here, on campus…"

"No, no, Linda. It's nothing like that. I've set up a solar test for this afternoon. Two o'clock is when the sun'll be right. I have it all programmed." He bent toward her and whispered, "This is much more than the test I showed you all on Saturday. This is the real thing. The real thing I'm working on. I haven't shown it to anyone else." He paused. "I'd like to show you what I'm really doing with the sun."

She clasped her hands and sighed, then looked up at him. "What are you talking about, Professor? You're scaring me a little."

He grabbed her hands. "Linda, I had a great time with you. Don't worry; no obligation on your part at all. I just want to show someone my real work. And I'd like it to be you."

Her smile came back. "I'd be real interested in that, Professor. Real interested in seeing the real thing. Let me run home and make some calls and get cleaned up." She moved her hands to hold and lightly caress his. "If it's as good as you say, maybe we'll celebrate again."

He smiled. "That would be great. But we don't have time for you to go home. It's all set for two o'clock; that's when the sun's in the right position." He looked at his watch. "That's just a little over an hour. I'm parked right here in the faculty lot. We'll go in my car. I can get you back whenever you need."

For a moment her eyes showed indecision, but then she nodded and let him steer her toward the parking lot. "Okay, let's do it, Professor." She looked around. "Which car?"

"The black Lexus. That's mine."

CHAPTER 12
MAKING GOLD

Forty-five minutes later, Linda Chavez and Professor Conan stood in front of his workbench. He had talked very little on the ride, saying he wanted to surprise her. A small stainless-steel pan rested on the wide windowsill that ran along the top of the bench. Above the sill was a large sliding window. It was ten minutes before two.

He leaned against the bench. "You've heard of alchemists, haven't you, Linda?"

"Sure. You mention them sometimes in class. Since ancient times, they've been trying to make gold out of lead, like some form of witchcraft. Dark chambers with steaming pots and flickering candles. All chasing dreams, if you ask me."

He smiled as he dropped a small pellet of lead into the pan on the windowsill. From a shelf below, he pulled up a plastic cup containing yellow shavings.

"These are gold shavings, Linda. About two grams. Authentic, traditional gold from old jewelry. Eventually, I'll add the shavings to the lead. The lead weighs about seventeen grams. When the process finishes,

I'll have made gold. Not only the two grams of gold that I start with, but a full nineteen grams. It'll all be gold. And after the small adjustment I'm making today, it'll be indistinguishable from real gold. It'll look the same, weigh the same, and be the same."

"No way, Professor. No way you can do that." She stepped back from the bench and stared at him. "Can you?"

He waved his arm around the room. "Just the opposite of dark rooms with steaming caldrons. I'm going to make gold, Linda. I'm going to turn lead into gold. The key element: the sun. The bright, full rays of the sun. You can't just heat the lead and the gold. The lead has to be touched by the sun; the solar rays have to touch and melt the metal. That is what people over the centuries missed; they overlooked the majesty of the actual embrace by the sun's rays." He smiled at her. "They also overlooked that alchemy is more than a process, Linda. It's a religion. To me, it's my soul."

He opened a drawer and pulled out Newton's journal, tapping it with his finger. "I found this old journal years ago. It contains a poem that says the sun must *touch matter as it lies,* actually touch the lead. That sent me in the right direction, and after years of more work and effort, I succeeded. I've turned lead into gold."

His chest puffed as he spoke and held up the journal. "It's where I learned the secret, Linda. The journal of Sir Isaac Newton, the greatest alchemist of them all." He smiled even bigger. "Until me, that is." He stood up straight. "I am now the greatest alchemist of them all, Linda. I took Newton's secret and perfected it." He watched her reaction. "I am the first man in the history of the world to make gold. I am a king."

"Why are you telling me all this, Professor, showing me all this?" she asked in a trembling voice. "You're scaring me a little again."

"Because you deserve to know, Linda. But wait, here comes the sunbeam. Right on time. Directly onto the lead to melt it; then I'll add the gold shavings. Then, at the right time, we'll move quickly outside and cool the mixture in pure running water. Watch closely. No one else has ever witnessed this. Up till now, it's been seen only by me."

Thirty minutes later, Conan pulled a ceramic mold from the stream of water outside the window and dropped a small yellow cube into his hand.

"This is gold, Linda. Pure, twenty-four-karat gold."

"Gosh, Professor. This is amazing. I don't know what to say. I can't believe it." She stared at the gold cube. "I think I need some time for it to sink in. Could you take me home? I'm sort of in shock."

"Of course I'll take you home." He lifted his finger. "But first, a toast. To my first witness." He pulled a wine bottle from his small lab refrigerator. "I have a special bottle of pinot. I already opened it so it can breathe. Before I take you home, a drink and a toast to what we've done. We've made gold today. Here, take this nugget we made. It's yours. My gift to you for everything you've done."

She sipped the glass that he poured, raising her eyes over the rim to him. "I haven't done anything, Professor."

"Oh, yes, Linda, you've done more than you realize. Here, drink up, and I'll take you home."

⚜

Linda Chavez woke up two hours later, strapped to a chair with duct tape. It was a wooden deck chair with wide, flat arms. Each of her wrists was taped to an arm, and her ankles were bound to the legs. Tape also sealed her mouth. Her eyes looked around the room. She saw a figure sitting in the shadows. The man stood when he saw her begin to stir.

"My dear Linda, I'm so glad you're back with us." He held up a hand as if she could interrupt him. "No need to say a thing." He smiled grimly. "I know. A dry mouth, a headache, a bit groggy. Just like I felt Sunday morning after you drugged me. Relax and gather your thoughts. Then we'll talk." He walked out of the room, pulling the door shut.

CHAPTER 13
WEDNESDAY'S TEAM MEETING

"I can't sign this," Mackie said as she looked up from the sheet of paper.

"Why the hell not!" Perkins shot back.

"Because it's a bunch of lies," she answered. "And I'm not going to sign an affidavit with a bunch of lies to get a subpoena."

Perkins stood and started to pace. "Look, Mackie, most affidavits are a bunch of lies. This one's truer than most."

"What? That I've traced a bunch of counterfeit currency to a black Lexus 460?" She stood and faced him. "You call that true?"

"Truer than most, damn it. Just sign it and let's get this thing going. We have a judge waiting. He won't even read the thing."

"I don't sign lies, Mr. Perkins. And it doesn't matter who you are or who you report to."

He stared at her, began to say more, then grabbed the paper from her and turned to leave, shouting, "Fine, Miss Holier-than-thou! It'll be redone for someone else's signature. It will be done. You all stay right here. I'll be back."

The room stayed coldly silent till he reentered. He paced the room then sat.

Mackie was still standing. "Before that came up, I did have a couple of suggestions."

"So what are they?"

"Since my field team is more or less grounded till we find the car, I've been spending more time on the mission book and doing some of my own research. Over the last few years, there have been a lot more than just private purchases of gold. A lot's been bought by governments and large banks."

"So what are you suggesting, Agent?" Perkins responded with a twist of his head and a smug look. "That we write letters to everyone, asking them to test their gold?"

She ignored him and faced the rest of the team. "No, a little more subtle than that. Most of our gold is stored at Fort Knox or the Federal Reserve in Manhattan. Fort Knox is our gold. Much of the gold at the Federal Reserve is actually owned by foreign countries. We just store it for them. I suggest we send a small team to do some testing of recent gold purchases at both places."

"Agent Mackie," Perkins exploded. "We're not going to test gold held by the United States Treasury under any circumstance. It's sacrosanct."

"Why's that, sir?" asked Cartwright.

"Because…because…just because. We're not going to question the full faith and credit of our bullion reserves."

Eyebrows rose around the room, and they glanced sideways at each other.

"Well, then, what about the banks, sir? The biggest locally is First National Bank of Miami. It holds a lot of gold bullion. It's purchased a lot in the last year."

"Where'd you get this information, Mackie?"

"I gave it to her," answered Cartwright. "We are a team, right?"

"Of course we're a team," Perkins replied. "But I'm the head of the team. I want to know what's going on. Everything. Always."

Mackie sat and shook her head. "Okay, John, you now know what's going on. What about the bank? I can get in with Ceshire with almost no publicity."

Perkins swallowed and gathered himself, then added calmly, "The only thing we're authorized to do is find who's making this new gold. Let me make it very clear." He looked around the room. "We do not care who has what gold."

Eyebrows went up again.

"We find this Henry David, and we stop him. That's our assignment. Period. Amen."

His phone rang.

"Yeah?…Good. Get it done."

He smiled and announced, "The affidavit's on its way. We'll have the names tomorrow. Then we go to work." He turned on his heel and left.

Mackie turned to her partner, shaking her head. "Why's he such an asshole, Michael?"

"He's just the messenger, Kate," he answered quietly. "Just the messenger."

"Well, I'm not just going to sit on my hands while he waits for the next message," she said. "A lot of countries are issuing commemorative gold coins, including Israel. I can buy them at jewelry stores—American Eagles, Maple Leafs, Krugerrands. We have funding, don't we, Madeline?"

The older woman nodded an affirmative.

"I'm going out to buy some gold coins." She looked at Doug Meyer. "Will you test their weight if I bring them in?"

"Definitely."

"I'll be back in a few hours." She stood and headed for the door.

The Israeli stood with her, but she shook her head. "I think I should be alone on this. Makes me look more like a collector, and"—she jerked her thumb at the door through which Perkins had just exited—"then he can blame only me."

"Sure. No problem," he answered. "But let's talk briefly outside. I might be able to help."

Once outside the building, he pulled his wallet out and withdrew a thin gold coin.

"Here's one of ours, hot off the press, issued this year. And if he doesn't destroy it in the testing, keep it. Remember, I promised you one."

She looked at the coin and fingered it gently. "Thanks. That saves Uncle Sam one purchase. They're awfully small, aren't they?"

That afternoon, Michael Bent sent another message: *Agent Mackie is purchasing national bullion coins to have them tested. I have provided her an Israeli coin minted this year.*

When she returned two hours later, Mackie turned six coins over to the chemist. She explained to him, "For each country, I purchased one issued this year and one from about ten years ago. For Israel, the oldest I could go was 2010, when they started issuing them."

"I'll give you a report before tomorrow's meeting," Meyer said as he took the coins. "Good to have something to do."

CHAPTER 14

THE INTERROGATION

She shivered; she prayed; and to her embarrassment, she wet her pants. She tasted bile but choked back the vomit, knowing there was nowhere for it to go with her mouth taped shut. After what seemed an eternity, Conan returned and stood in front of her, his hands clasped at his waist. He stared at her bound body.

"Okay, Linda, we need to talk. I'll take the tape off your mouth, but if you scream or misbehave, it'll go back on. Then we'll have nothing to talk about." He stood in front of her, as she nodded, sad but resigned. "Do you understand the rules?"

She closed her eyes and nodded again.

He grabbed her head with one hand and pulled the tape off her mouth with the other, leaving a strip of tape hanging down the right side of her face. Conan stepped back, stroking his chin, and stared at his prisoner.

"Who are you, Linda? Why were you here?"

She sat silently, shivering from fear and her wetness, sensing she was going to die. Why talk?

"You're going to kill me anyway," she sobbed. "I knew when you showed me all that stuff this afternoon, I was in trouble. You were just toying with me. You wouldn't show me everything and then let me leave. Please, please, let me go. I'll do whatever you want."

"Linda, what I want is to know how much you learned, how much you've compromised me. Why were you here? I'm not a killer. I don't want to hurt you. But you have to talk."

"They'll be here," she whispered vehemently, tears running down her face. "They'll probably be here any minute. And you'll be in a lot of trouble."

"Linda, no one knows you're here. We left from the sidewalk, remember? You didn't have a chance to tell anyone where you were going. That was my plan. Assuming you're a foreigner, my guess is you're an illegal. No one's going to miss you. If they do, there's nothing to lead them here. But that's enough of this."

He pulled a jack knife out of his pocket and opened the blade. *Here comes the hard part,* he thought. *Have to do this to make her take me seriously.* He drew the blade across her left arm. They both watched a line of blood appear, which grew as it curled around and down her arm.

He became stern. "I've spent my entire life working toward this moment. Hours and hours and years and years. You can't even imagine. You're not going to walk in here and fuck me and steal my secrets." He pointed at her arm. "That blood is like a magnet for alligators, wild pigs, and other things right across the road. You either tell me what's going on or I'll take you there right now. Don't make me a killer, Linda. Tell me what's happening."

She believed him, so she talked. At least it would buy time. Maybe someone would come. "I'm from Cuba. They sent me to find out if you knew how to make gold. They are very interested."

"Cuba? Why Cuba? Who are they? How do they know about me?"

"I don't know. They told me you wrote an article in some magazine which our president read. Fidel and his brother have practiced the witchcraft Santería for years. I guess its customs have ties to your alchemy, but I really don't know. They want to make gold, both to fulfill their imaginations and to upset the world. So they hired me to get your secrets." She sobbed, panting for breath. "Could I have some water, something to drink?"

"We'll see, Linda. Maybe after you tell me everything." Conan rubbed his eyes and cocked his head. "So Cuba wants to make gold. Wants *me* to make gold." He nodded. "I did publish an article. That was a year ago, before I knew I could do it. I knew it was stupid to write, but I was cocky. Thought I could make a little splash and not reveal too much." He shook his head, now talking to himself. "Shit, why didn't I just keep my mouth shut?" He leaned closer. "What did you tell them?"

"They know everything that was in your computer and have copies of your papers. So they know you've either done it or are very close."

"Well, I know you didn't find my journal, so they don't know everything. Who exactly are they and what's next?"

She sat with her eyes closed then opened them and looked at him. "They are the Black Wasps. I don't know what's next," she murmured, her head drooping. "I was just given the assignment. I thought I could soon go home. Please, Professor, we could go to Cuba and you could be a national hero. I could go with you. Make you happy."

"Yeah. I'd be happy till you stuck a knife in my back. And as you said, they'd destroy the world order with my work. I don't want that." He paused. "Who the hell are the Black Wasps?"

"It's their special forces. They are very bad people. They are probably here by now." She looked up at him. "What do you want, Professor? I'm begging. I'll do anything. They will come here. If I'm here, I can help you. If you hurt me, they'll hurt you."

"If they come here, they won't find much," he answered almost absentmindedly. "My secrets are now well hidden. They'll find only a professor heating water with sunlight."

She tried one last time, lifting her face to him and pleading. "What do you want, Professor? I can do even more for you than before."

He strode up, grabbed her shoulders and shook her. "I want to be left alone to make gold! And when I'm ready, I'll go public in a way that anoints me a king of history. And I won't destroy the world financial order like your two-bit dictator would if he got my secrets. And no, you cannot help me, Linda."

He let go of her shoulders and turned, almost crying, "Why have you made me do this? Why didn't you just…mind your own business?!"

She sobbed. She knew all was lost.

"I'll get you some water." He walked away. "I'll put something in it. You won't feel anything."

Conan walked to his study and sat with his head back and eyes closed. What could he do? A painful grimace froze his face as he tried to decide. If he released her, his journey was over. She would tell everything, and now she knew everything. It had been stupid to show her how to make gold. Why had he done that? But he couldn't kill her. He just couldn't do that.

"Henry David," his mother had often lectured, "you do what is necessary to finish the assignment. You are never too weak or tired to finish. You do what is necessary."

He got up and walked to the kitchen to get her a glass of water, into which he shook the remaining powder from the vial in his pocket. Returning to Linda, he helped her drink.

Soon she was unconscious again. He cut the tape and pulled her body to the floor, where he retaped her hands, feet, and mouth. He didn't want any screaming. Since she was too heavy for him to carry, he dragged her by her feet to the deck, wincing each time her head bounced on the wooden floorboards. *Here's where she started it*, he remembered. *She got me to let my guard down here on the deck. And now I have to get rid of her. There's just no other way. It's all her fault. I'm just defending myself.* Professor Conan nodded to convince himself it was so; he was acting in self-defense.

From the deck, he rolled her body into the right side of the golf cart seat, got in, and drove toward the marsh across the street. He'd go at least a couple of miles, and she'd be alive when he left her. He wouldn't be the killer.

I'm not killing her, he continued to say. *She's killing herself. She and the Black Wasps, whoever they are.* With no headlights, he could barely see the light-colored path through the swamp. He had positioned her body to lean back, but one big bump made her body fall sideways onto his lap. Her eyes were open, staring up at him. He shivered uncontrollably.

This is it, as far as I'm going to go, he screamed to himself. He yanked the wheel to turn around, having to turn three times to get around in the narrow space. When in reverse, the cart beeped loudly, and he cringed with each beep, sure that someone would hear it. He pushed her body over the side. He knew he should roll her off the road, but he couldn't touch her again. He fled to his house.

"What have I done? What have I done?" he cried to the skies.

CHAPTER 15
THURSDAY'S TEAM MEETING

"We have a fucking leak!" Perkins yelled at the group. "Someone's putting information out."

"What do you mean?" asked Madeline Cartwright. "Why do you think there's a leak?"

"Because yesterday morning Cuba announced a multi-year deal to give Saudi Arabia exclusive rights to operate the Cuban gold mine in the Orient region. In return, they're getting a ten-year supply of crude for their new Havana oil refinery. The deal was priced at current gold prices."

"How does that become a leak?" queried John Ceshire.

"Because a guy by the name of Ivan Martinez, Cuba's vice minister of basic industries, was asked about the deal and said,"—he read off a paper in his hand—"'Why keep our gold if there might someday be an abundance of cheap gold?'" He looked up, his face bright red. "The guy's only a couple of hundred miles from here. We're looking for someone in south Florida who's making gold, and this asshole in Cuba says there might soon be a lot of cheap gold. Pretty goddamned big coincidence, wouldn't you say?"

He glared around the room. "And they didn't do this deal with their great partner and ally, Venezuela, which would be natural if it was a straight deal. No, they went to the Saudis. So if the price of gold tanks and Saudi Arabia gets pissed, which they will, they won't have alienated their real friends. And you know what happened last night?" He slashed a line from top to bottom on the chalkboard behind him. "The price of gold plummeted. Spot prices declined fifteen percent within hours of that news flash. In China and India there are panicky lines at all the jewelry and gem stores. People are trying to sell their hoarded gold—at any price. Folks, there's a gold panic taking place. And I suspect the leak came from someone in this room."

"What about this Martinez guy?" asked Mackie. "Anything more from him?"

"Things are suddenly real quiet down in Cuba," said Perkins. "Martinez is nowhere to be found, and the government has issued a statement saying, essentially, he's nuts. So things will probably quiet down, but this shows what can happen if news gets out about this new gold."

He scanned the table with accusing eyes. "I want to know who you've been talking to. And I have an FBI polygraph team outside. You're all taking a lie-detector test. We will get to the bottom of this."

"How about you, sir?" Mackie asked quietly.

"What? What about me?"

"Are you taking a polygraph, sir?"

"No, I'm not taking a goddamned polygraph test, Agent Mackie. And I've had just about enough from you. Maybe you should be first in line. And you can explain your jewelry shop purchases yesterday, which just might have been the leak."

"I'd be happy to take the first test, sir. But I think you should be tested, too. Sometimes unintentional leaks surface during these tests." She stood and stared at him without blinking. "And as for the cheap shot about my coin purchases, you'll see from the paperwork that they all took place after three o'clock yesterday afternoon." She stuck out her hand. "Could I see that release?" He shoved it to her, and she looked at it. "As you said, and as this confirms, Martinez made his statement at ten o'clock yesterday morning. Sort of tough for what I did at three in the afternoon to cause a news release five hours earlier."

Perkins glared. People at the table held their smiles.

"And my coin purchases did reveal an anomaly."

Speaking stiffly through tight lips, Perkins said, "What do you mean, an anomaly?"

"Meyer tested the coins last night. Here's his report." She handed two pages to him. "Five of the six coins weighed in as pure, old-fashioned twenty-four-karat gold." She picked up a document from the table and continued. "One, however, was too light."

"Which one?" Perkins asked.

"Let me explain first." She looked over at Michael Bent, who sat next to her. "Michael was good enough to provide me with a new Jerusalem gold coin issued this year. It tested fine. But my approach was to compare new coins with older ones. I bought another Jerusalem coin from the first issue year, 2010. This report says the older coin was light."

Bent looked up and shrugged, open palms above the table. "I have no idea how that could happen."

Perkins also looked confused. "Makes no sense to me."

"There is at least one explanation," Mackie said, turning again to look at her partner.

"Don't hold us all in suspense, Agent Mackie," snapped Perkins.

She took a deep breath and leaned forward. "Someone in Israel might have gotten better at making gold."

CHAPTER 16
THE IMPOSTER

Kate Mackie heard from Jonathon that evening. She saw the caller i.d. before picking up the phone and remembered how they had first met when she was still at the White House. Running on a Sunday morning, she had come up behind him and started to pass. He saw her and picked up his pace. Soon it was a race, one which he later claimed he had let her win. Gasping on their backs on the grass afterward, they learned that they had each grown up in Boston, she from the poor Dorchester section and he from the elite of Cambridge. A few dates led to a relationship, after he had been cleared by the Secret Service. Every friend, associate, and lover had to be cleared to ensure they weren't a burrowing mole. It was embarrassing to report a friend—much less a potential lover—but she'd done it. And per regulation, she hadn't told him. He passed.

Now they were fifteen hundred miles apart, and she was eating takeout alone, listening to her favorite jazz, and reading about gold.

"Hi, Kate. This is your ex-lover and boyfriend, the one you stood up for vacation."

"Oh, Jon, stop that stuff. We're not ex anything…are we?"

"No, I guess not. Just my dark humor. I did manage to cancel just about everything, and the hotel's giving us a full refund as long as we rebook. We will rebook, won't we?"

"Yes. We'll rebook and it'll be even greater than we planned. I'll need a vacation after putting up with this guy down here. He's a real asshole."

"Now, Agent Mackie, be careful with your language. They hear everything."

"Yeah, they probably do. Hopefully, he'll kick me off the team. We don't exactly see eye to eye."

"Well, I have some answers for you. And some information on your friend down there. First, my research tells me that there's nothing wrong with making metal—any metal. It's done every day. As long as it's the real thing and not some cheap imitation passed off as authentic, nothing wrong with making copper or aluminum or anything else."

"Make any difference how valuable the metal is?"

"Shouldn't. No laws saying you can't make metals. I found it's a federal crime to make gold coins which resemble official currency, but that would be a stretch today since gold isn't official currency anymore. But remember, the stuff has to be authentic. If it's not and if someone passes it off as the real thing, it's at least fraud."

She held the phone away from her ear for a moment to think and then brought it back. "Sorry, I got distracted. That's helpful, I think. What about my buddy?"

"Now that, Kate, is a paradox. I was talking to a friend at the Department of Justice yesterday and mentioned that one John Perkins of Justice had just ruined my vacation. Stolen my girlfriend—"

"I'm not sure that was a good idea."

"Maybe not, but it got me some interesting information…if you want it."

"Don't tease. What'd he say?"

"Said there's no John Perkins in any senior position at Justice."

"What? That can't be so. He's here. He's running the show. He's a big gun."

"This guy's been at Justice for five years. He's on the human resource side. He assures me there's no such animal there."

"So who the hell is this John Perkins? And what kind of a mess am I in?"

"Wait, I have more. My friend called me back last night. Said he had made some inquiries. Said this guy is not with the Department of Justice but is associated with another agency. Wouldn't tell me anything more. Said to remember we never had the conversation. He would deny it."

"Jesus, Jonathon. So what's the other agency?"

"I think we both know. And if he's CIA, he shouldn't be involved in domestic activities, if that's what you're doing."

"Yeah, it's domestic."

"What are you going to do, Kate?"

"I have no idea. You tell me my boss is an imposter. He has me working, maybe unlawfully, on this project. I have no idea what to do."

"You have to get out."

"You're right, but then they'd just trash me and replace me. I think I have to find out what's going on."

"Kate, these are big, bad guys. If you get in their way, they'll hurt you."

"I know, I know. But I can't just walk away." She drummed her fingers on her chair as she thought. "I think I'm going to contact President Menton. She gave me her personal email. Told me to reach out if I ever needed her help. I sure need help."

"She's an ex-president, dear. What can she do?"

"I don't know. But she knows a lot of people; she's seen a lot, has good judgment. It's a shot in the dark, but it's all I can think of. So I'm going to do that, and I'll let you know what she says."

"Why don't I fly down to Miami to give you some support? I can be there tomorrow."

"No. Thanks for offering, but I have to do this myself. And until I figure out what's going on, I still have this assignment. I'll be out in the field tomorrow, chasing some leads. I'm going to send that email right now. Thanks so much, for everything, and for not being mad. I will make it up to you."

After hanging up, Kate went into her contacts list and found the email address the president had given her. She hadn't used it before. She flashed back to the meeting in the Oval Office two years before, when President Menton had promoted her to the presidential Secret Service protection team from the U.S. Marshals Service. Those had been heady times. She hoped the President would remember her. She typed, hesitated, then hit send.

President Menton,

You said I could contact you if I ever needed help. I need your advice, and your help. I apologize for bothering you, but could you call me at your earliest convenience at the following number?

CHAPTER 17
TEAM MEETING

"Folks, we have the Lexus names," announced John Perkins as he distributed two-page lists to the group. "Haven't even looked at them yet. Just came in."

Six heads bent to read the names.

"Looks like about fifty names over in Collier and Lee counties," murmured John Ceshire.

"And look at the third down on the second page," exclaimed Mackie. "Henry D. Conan. What do you want to bet the D. stands for David?" She looked up with a frown. "The son of a bitch used most of his own name. Maybe not as smart a guy as we thought. It's a Fort Myers address."

"We're out of here," said Michael Bent, pushing back his chair to stand. "Mackie and I can be in Fort Myers in an hour if we go hot, and we're going hot. Our GPS will give us the directions. Look into this guy and call us with what you find." The two of them rushed from the room.

"Mind if I drive this time?" he asked as they got in the elevator.

"Be my guest," Mackie said. "I'll work the phone."

Mackie's phone rang before they were on I-75. She punched the speaker key.

"It's *Professor* Henry David Conan," blared Perkins. "Florida Gulf Coast University, environmental sciences, no record, no violations, no nothing. The address is a bit of a problem. We brought it up on the map. He's right on the Caloosahatchee River, and it looks like a long, wide-open private road to his driveway. There's no way you can get close without being seen. What? What is it, John?... Fine, okay. Ceshire says he has something important. We're all here on the line."

"Yeah, Ceshire here. I've come up with something. I put in place a media search program to catch every mention of the word *gold* in newspapers or on the news. Got a very unusual hit this morning."

"What is it?" said Mackie. "What's the hit?"

"Small blurb in this morning's *News-Press* from Fort Myers. Seems a body was found in the Everglades, east of Fort Myers. It was pretty well mangled by animals."

"So what does that have to do with gold?" yelled Bent as he roared onto I-75 and hit ninety miles an hour. "What's the big deal about a dead body?"

Ceshire's voice came back. "The headline read, 'Body with a gold nugget.' There was a gold nugget in the corpse's pocket. And there's something else. I called and got the location where they found the body. Hunters found it off a power line right-of-way hunters use to get into the swamp."

Perkins jumped in. "Is there more?"

"Yeah. One more point. The right of way begins across the street from this guy's driveway."

The silence that followed was broken by Mackie. "Maybe not such an innocent professor, after all." She thought for a moment. "Meyer, you there?"

"I'm here."

"Can you do a quick field test on that gold nugget? Get over to Fort Myers and weigh it, measure it, and whatever else is necessary. Find out whether it's some of this new gold."

"Sure. I can do that. I'm on my way."

"Remember, guys," spoke Perkins over the phone, "I want a quiet approach once we know he's home. I want to surprise him. Don't go in with guns blazing."

When Mackie and Bent exited I-75 in Fort Myers, he slowed to the speed limit. Their car was unmarked, but the state troopers had been alerted and hadn't stopped them as they sped across the state. Local roads were another story. They took Route 80 east till the GPS directed them over the Caloosahatchee. As they took the bridge over the river, Bent pulled over and they peered to the right—where they thought Conan's home was located. A small commercial marina spanned the bank under the bridge.

"Jesus," Mackie sighed once they reached the access road. "Might as well be a castle surrounded by a moat. There's no way to get close to that place undetected. If he wanted privacy, he got it. Look!" She pointed to their left at power lines and a dirt road running under them. "That's the right-of-way where they found the body." She looked to the right. "And that's his driveway. Just as John said. Right across the street."

"I'll turn around and head back across the river," said the Israeli. "We'll find a spot to watch the place. Maybe see what his schedule is. Don't even know if he's home." He looked at his watch. "It's two o'clock. I think we have to go in at night, probably on the river, and we'll have to assemble some gear and backup. I don't think we can be ready by tonight. Probably tomorrow. Let's look at this marina. We could get kayaks and go in from here. It's only about half a mile to his dock."

CHAPTER 18

PRESIDENTIAL DECEPTION

"Hello?"

"President Menton?"

"Who is this?"

"John Perkins, ma'am. I'm a special assistant to the attorney general, Department of Justice."

"How'd you get this number, Mr. Perkins? It's a private number."

"Well, ma'am, as you know, there's not too much that's really private these days. I'm sorry to bother you, but we think you've recently received a communication from one of our agents which was unauthorized. I'm calling to explain an email Agent Kathryn Mackie sent you."

"Mr. Perkins—if that is your name—I'm not about to discuss my emails with you or anyone else. You say you're an assistant to the attorney general, Howard Abbott?"

"Yes, ma'am. I report to Mr. Abbott. We're involved in a sensitive national security matter. Agent Mackie is on a government team instructed to maintain absolute secrecy. We detected her recent email to you. I don't know why she sent it, but we want to assure you that there is no need for you to contact her."

"Tell you what, Mr. Perkins. I appointed Howard Abbott attorney general. He's a holdover from my administration. Good friend. I'll talk to him about this matter. Not to you. And, Mr. Perkins…"

"Yes, ma'am?"

"You delete this number from your database. I'm going to find out how you got it, and you'd better not use it again. Do we understand each other, Mr. Perkins?"

"Fully, ma'am. I'll ask the attorney general to contact you."

"That won't be necessary, sir. I know how to reach him."

CHAPTER 19
A NIGHTTIME INTRUSION

Mackie and Bent found a place to park on the riverbank at the rear of a large trailer park. With binoculars, they had a good view of Conan's house. They saw no activity, and a call to the house was not answered. They placed more calls to line up equipment and backup for the next night. At six, they observed a black Lexus drive down the access road and turn into the driveway. One man got out of the car and entered the house. He fit the description they had been given.

"This is frustrating," she exclaimed as she watched Professor Conan walk into his house. "He's right there. He delivered the bad gold, so I'm guessing he also made it. And that dead woman was found right across the street from his house. I think we should move in."

"Kate, we can't. He'll have at least a minute's warning if we drive in, with or without headlights. And if he can make gold, I imagine he knows about motion detectors and security devices. Look at those towers." He pointed and handed her the glasses. "My guess is they're high-tech motion detectors. We get close, he'll be warned. Perkins says it has to be a surprise entry."

"Yeah, Perkins," she said with disgust as she faced her partner. "I can't figure him out. I'm not sure if he really wants this guy. He's certainly throwing up roadblocks."

"Oh, I think he wants him," Bent answered with a shrug. "Just wants it done his way."

Their phone rang.

"Mackie here." She listened for a moment. "What? Really? Could there be any mistake?…Just surprises me.…Yeah, you're right. He could have gotten better.… That's right." She turned to Bent. "Just like the Israelis. Talk to you later." She hung up. "That was Doug Meyer. Guess what, Michael? The nugget found on the body doesn't weigh the traditional nineteen point three grams or the new nineteen. It's nineteen point two."

"That's a pretty small discrepancy. Maybe a mistake?"

"Meyer swears that it's no mistake. This is closer to real gold, but still not there. He says the guy made it. And one other thing."

"What?"

"The corpse is female, and although she might have been killed by the animals, there were traces of duct tape on her wrists and ankles." She nodded to herself. "I want to get this son of a bitch. He left this lady out in the swamp to be killed and eaten by gators and pigs. Meyer says the preliminary autopsy says she was alive when she was dropped there. She was eaten alive, Michael. The bastard left her out there to be eaten alive. Probably thought she'd never be found."

Bent squeezed her shoulder. "We're going to get him. But it has to be tomorrow night. We'll watch the place tonight. Make sure nothing else happens. If there's anything unusual, we'll go in sooner."

⁂

Mackie and Bent arrived at the marina at nine o'clock the next night, and packed their gear and weapons into two kayaks they had rented. The marina was quiet and dark. They carried the kayaks to the bottom of the boat ramp where a low but full moon cast their shadows onto the river as they worked. Kate had copied Bent's usual black dress code. Bent had also blackened his face. Mackie's already dark complexion made that unnecessary.

"What's all the gear, Michael?" she asked, watching him stuff two backpacks into the rear compartment of his kayak. She walked over to see for herself. The distinctive orange package was obvious. "That's Semtex. Why the hell do you have Semtex? We're not going to blow anything up."

"It's extra ammunition and stuff I always carry." He looked up. "I like to be ready for anything." He clamped the hatch cover shut. As he stood, he spit into the water and pushed some seeds into his mouth.

"What are those?" she asked. "What are you chewing?"

"These?" He raised his hand and tossed a handful of seeds. "Just sunflower seeds. Good for energy. Always chew them on a mission. Sort of a habit. Here." He dropped a few into her hand. "Try a few but don't swallow the hulls; spit those out."

"That's okay," she said, putting them back into his hand. "Thanks anyway. But gee, do you really want to be carrying explosives?"

"It's perfectly harmless unless I put a charge to it."

"And I guess you have charge caps also?"

He stood still. "As I said, I carry enough gear to be ready for anything. It's how I work."

She shrugged. "Let's get in the water. The FBI team's going to stay at the intersection unless we call," she reminded him, as if they hadn't talked it all through. "Perkins says that if things go smoothly, he isn't even going to involve them. We'll go ashore at ten, the time when he turned off the lights last night. He should be alone, so there shouldn't be any problem, unless he has motion detectors."

"If the professor has security," Bent said, "it'll be on the road side. He doesn't expect visitors from the river. I think we'll be fine. Okay, we're set. Keep the back of the kayak on the ramp as you get in; then push off with your hands. Don't want to tip these things."

"Think there are any alligators in the river?" She pushed out with her hands.

"Probably not. Too much salt this close to the Gulf. But I'm still happy in a kayak rather than swimming."

They paddled upstream and across the river, their boats side by side, ten feet apart, with Mackie on the left. They wanted darkness but the moon wasn't cooperating, and moon rays shimmered across the water. They saw lights blinking on the shore and vehicles moving along the bridge. The first fifty yards were under the bridge, where the clatter of the tires overhead was deafening. Once they paddled away from the bridge, the rumble stopped, and it became quiet. They set their eyes on the small dock in front of Conan's house. About halfway to their destination, they heard guttural bellowing from the shore on their right.

"Guess there are some gators around," the Israeli whispered over to her. Then the distinctive hoo-hoo call of an owl came from the trees.

"The lights are still on," she whispered as they approached the dock. They were close to shore, still side by side. He nodded and pointed to a boat floating near the dock. He signaled with hand gestures that he was going to check out the boat. She pulled for shore.

"Forget the lights," he whispered back. "We're doing this."

CHAPTER 20
THE CUBAN INVASION

Professor Conan watched one of his gangster movies. At home he didn't worry about his elevated shoes and pressed pants. He wore khakis, a golf shirt, and sandals. The movie was *Road to Perdition* with Paul Newman and Tom Hanks. In college, he had started collecting mob movies, and he had a large collection from the thirties to modern times. For some reason, he enjoyed the violence and brutality of the mobsters, so different from his own nonviolent ways. *At least his previous ways,* he thought.

A bottle of Willamette pinot noir stood ready to be uncorked. He was staying up, hoping his bartender friend Marge would stop by after work. She often did on Tuesdays when she got off work at PJ's Lounge at ten. He remembered first meeting her when he stopped for a drink on his way home one evening.

"What can I do for you, sir?" she had called out from behind the bar.

"Have any good red wine? A cab or a pinot?"

She leaned on the bar in front of him. "Sir, you might be in the wrong place if you're looking for a good red wine." She leaned closer, showing straight white teeth. "Don't take me wrong, but look around at these guys." She pointed her thumbs in both directions. "They think zinfandel is a Christmas jingle. I can get you a nice cold beer or cheap whiskey, but you really don't want to drink my wine."

The beer was cold, and they struck up a conversation. After a few more visits, they were on a first-name basis, and he explained that he lived across the river.

One night he took a gamble. "You know, Marge, I do have some good red wine at my place. If you want to stop over after work, I'll open a bottle."

Her eyes widened and her body stiffened.

"Just a glass of wine," he quickly added. "That's all."

She came over a few times. They watched one of his movies and drank some wine. That was all. She was a good listener and smart, and he enjoyed her company.

His reverie was suddenly shattered.

"Señor Conan," boomed a voice from the doorway as two men strode into his living room. "We are here to find out what happened to Linda. And to learn more about your gold."

He jumped up to confront them but was grabbed by his shoulders from behind and thrown back to the chair.

"You stay right there," the man ordered. "You stay right there and answer our questions."

"Who the hell are you?" yelled the professor as he struggled against two strong hands holding him in the chair.

"Tie him," the man ordered. "Tie his hands and strap him to the chair. Who we are is unimportant." The leader stood in front of Conan while his companions bound him. "We have been sent to get information from you, and we will get it, or you will suffer much pain. First, we want to know what happened to your student and our friend Linda."

"I don't know what you're talking about," he spit out. "Just get out of my house."

"You know very well who I talk about, Professor." He pointed at the other two. "Search the place." He then squatted with his face inches from Conan's. "The woman you fucked a week ago. We visited her apartment today. It seems she disappeared—very suddenly. Her bed was unmade, dirty dishes in the sink; neighbors haven't seen her in three days."

Professor Conan's mind blurred as he tried to think. They can't really know anything about Linda. No one knows she was here. They're just guessing.

"Yes, I have a student of that name. She was here a week ago, along with the entire class. But I haven't seen her since. If she's done something wrong, I'm not involved. What are you doing here?"

"I think the professor is going to need some convincing." He nodded to one of his men and turned away. Conan jerked as he saw a woman walk through the door. Her smile turned into an open-mouthed scream when she saw Conan bound to the chair with strangers standing over him. The man pulled a pistol from his belt and clipped off two quick shots to her head. Her scream turned to a gurgle as she fell to the floor.

He turned back to Conan. "Who the hell is she?" he shouted, waving his pistol.

"Just a friend," cried Conan. "You've shot my friend. Oh my god. You killed her," he sobbed, tears running down his cheeks. "You killed Marge. Why did you do that?" he whimpered. "She was just a friend."

Mackie's kayak bumped the riverbank, and she lifted herself out with hands on the cockpit sides. Before she was out, a scream of terror split the night air, followed by two sharp blasts.

"That's from the house," she muttered, looking back for Bent. She didn't see him. Pushing herself up with her arms, she swung her legs out of the cockpit and into shallow water. The four-foot riverbank was no obstacle, and she was running toward the house in no time, pulling her pistol from its holster and keeping it at her side. She heard nothing, no more screams or shots. The lit house gave her a beacon. *That was a woman's scream,* she thought. *It stopped after the shots. Goddamn. Do we have another body?*

She covered the fifty yards in long, loping strides, looking for danger ahead but not making the careful approach she had been trained to do. She should have stopped at the corner of the house but she didn't. Instead, she rounded it at full speed, not at first seeing the man standing next to the front door. She detected movement and slowed, but it was too late.

Mackie's chest exploded as the shotgun slug hit her. She felt lightning flash through her head and a sledgehammer smash into her chest. She crumpled to the ground, unconscious before she hit.

Professor Conan heard another shot from outside, and soon a man rushed into the room and reported to the leader with gestures toward the front door. The leader turned to the professor.

"You seem to have another visitor, señor. Another woman. This one carried a gun." He slapped Conan across the face. "Stop the damn crying. Is this another friend? Are there any more we should expect?"

"I…don't…know…who she is," stammered the professor. "I don't know what's going on. Why don't you just leave me alone?"

"Oh, no, señor, we will not leave you alone." His cell rang and he pulled it to his ear. "Yeah?" He looked at Conan and cocked his head before speaking into the phone. "A third, heh, and this one a man? And another gun? A bunch of guns?… No, just tie them up. They might be the law. Get the boat ready. We'll talk a bit more with the professor then bring him to the boat. We should leave quickly.… I don't care if she's dead. You're not a fucking doctor. Tie her up so she doesn't come back from the dead."

CHAPTER 21
THE EX-PRESIDENT

"Howard, so glad to hear back from you. I was beginning to wonder if my favorite attorney general had forgotten who appointed him."

"Now, Madam President, don't be too tough. It's only been a day."

Yeah, a day to get a story right, she thought. *I checked; he was there yesterday.* With a bright, cheery voice, she said, "It's so seldom I can be tough anymore. And let's drop the 'Madam President' stuff. You seldom did that even when I was in office."

"You're right, Natalie. You be as tough as you want. So to what do I owe the privilege of hearing from our esteemed former president with a callback request of, if I'm reading correctly, extreme importance?"

"I might have exaggerated," she said with a chuckle. "I'm calling about a former protective agent of mine who I think is now working for one John Perkins of the Justice Department. She contacted me and seems to think something's wrong with the mission or Mr. Perkins or something I don't quite understand. Then yesterday morning I get a call on my very private line from a Mr. Perkins telling me to, essentially, butt out. Now,

Howard, as I think you know, I don't butt out very easily. And this lady—she's a woman—was very loyal and professional when she worked for me. I trusted her with my life. So I'm calling the top and maybe calling in a favor. I'd like to know what's going on. Believe it or not, I'm on a cruise ship in Asia taking a leisurely world tour—much more pleasant than those jaunts on Air Force One. The captain has loaned me his cabin and what he says is a secure phone line."

There was a pause on the line. She could swear there were some noises in the background.

"Sorry, Natalie, these international connections are sometimes bad even for me." Another pause. "I know this John Perkins. He's not exactly with the department, but, uh, I think he's working on a project under our auspices."

"Certainly wouldn't be CIA working domestically, would it, Howard? You know that's a no-no."

"I'm sure that's not so, Natalie, but I'm really not completely up to speed on his project. Who's this agent and what's she saying?"

"Kathryn Mackie's her name. All I have is an email saying she might need help. I haven't talked to her yet. Am I being ordered not to talk to her?"

"Of course not. You can talk to whomever you please. I assume she's under a secrecy blanket in the project, and if she's good, as you say, she's probably not going to tell you much. Wait one second. My aide's here for some reason."

Almost half a minute went by. "Sorry about that. They always think everything's so darn important."

No, she thought, *no one interrupts a private phone call of the United States attorney general unless it is darn important.*

He continued, "I've dealt with this Perkins in the past. He's a bit rough, has a reputation as a difficult guy to work for. I bet he's just giving her a hard time. But you've called the favor, and I'll find out what's going on. It might take a few days, but I'll get back to you."

"Can you tell me about their project?" she pushed.

"I'd probably get it all wrong. I think it has something to do with counterfeiting, since your friend is now on that side of the Service, but let me see what I can find out."

"I appreciate that, Howard. Please make sure she doesn't get trashed because of this. Kathryn Mackie's a good person."

Ex-president Menton put the phone down in the captain's suite, where she had been summoned to take it. Something bothered her. Something wasn't right. She thought through the conversation, then snapped her fingers and nodded sharply, muttering to herself, "How'd he know she was in counterfeiting? I didn't tell him. He knows a lot more than he's saying."

CHAPTER 22
ANOTHER INTERROGATION

The intruders' leader closed his phone and strode to face Professor Conan. He stood in front of the frightened man with hands on hips and spoke softly.

"We have too many visitors, señor, so we must move—quickly—without any more of your games. Linda Chavez can wait. But my orders are to get your journal, the one your notes sometimes describe as Newton's journal. Where is it?"

Conan blinked rapidly through eyes caked with dried tears. "I have no journal here," he gasped, hyperventilating with fear. "There is no journal."

The leader nodded to the man standing behind the chair. "Take his thumb. Whichever is easier."

"No," Conan murmured. "No…"

The man reached with his left arm, grabbed Conan's right hand, and raised it to the arm of the chair. With his right hand he pulled a twelve-inch machete from a thigh sheath and swiped it downward. Conan's thumb fell to the floor.

Conan's eyes went wide. At first, he felt very little pain. He saw his raw thumb stump spurting blood. Then his hand was on fire.

"My god!" he screamed. "What have you done? I'm going to bleed to death. Please, I need a doctor. You've ruined my hand," he sobbed. "You've ruined me."

"Don't worry, señor. We'll find a bandage, stop the bleeding…after you tell us where the journal is. Which is it, Professor? Bleed to death and maybe lose the other thumb, or tell us what we want?"

"I'll tell you everything." Conan's voice cracked. "Please don't hurt me anymore. The book's in a storage container I rented. In Fort Myers. Not too far from here. But you have to help me. You cut off my thumb!"

"Bandage the hand, Miguel. Then we'll go to this storage place."

Conan's head was shaking. "We can't go now. It's the middle of the night. It's not open now."

"When does it open, señor?"

"I think at seven," he whimpered.

The leader twirled his fingers to his men. "So we leave now. Get him to the boat and grab any papers in his office and his computer. We'll go back to the marina and wait till morning. Once we get the book, we continue our fishing charter." He smiled. "Out to the Gulf and southeast, to Havana. They don't care about boats going in that direction."

"What about my thumb?" Conan cried, trying to stop the bleeding by squeezing his right wrist with his left hand. "I need help."

"We'll wrap it with something, señor." He pointed to one of the men. "Go find some bandages or a towel. He'll live."

CHAPTER 23
BACK FROM THE DEAD

She woke coughing and spitting water through her nose and mouth. Her nose stung as the water spurted out. She was drowning. But she'd been shot. She shouldn't be drowning…unless it was in her own blood. Her eyes fluttered open, and she saw a man's face close to hers. He was spitting a stream of water into her face. It was Bent—Michael Bent.

"Michael! What the hell are you doing?" she stammered as she coughed up more water.

"Trying to wake you up," he said, spitting the remaining water onto the ground next to her.

"I was shot," she moaned, "in the chest." She looked up and grimaced. "I thought I was dead. Shit, my chest feels torn open."

"No. I checked. No penetration. Your vest did its job."

He straightened and she saw he was on his knees, his hands tied behind his back. Hers were tied at her waist.

"But we're tied up like trussed chickens," he said. "We have to get out of here and find these guys. I've been spitting river water in your face.

Was able to suck it up out of that wooden trough." He nodded his head to the water basin Conan used to cool the gold. "Figured it'd either wake you or drown you."

Her eyes closed as pain shot across her chest. "Well, it hurts to wake up. But I guess it's better than the alternative. How'd they get you?"

"Was trying to follow you, but I saw that boat idling without lights just off his dock. Checked it out quickly then beached it. Last I remember, I was getting my gear out of the kayak. Someone hit me with something." He turned his head from side to side as if testing it. "Lucky I have a hard head. But let's forget this chitchat. We need to get out of here and find these guys. The professor's either dead or they took him."

"You don't think they were his security?"

"No way. Much too aggressive for private security." He rolled to his back and kicked his legs over her body. "I think my knife's still in my ankle sheath. Try to pull it out and cut whatever's around my wrists. Sorry, didn't mean to hurt you," he added as he saw her wince when his legs hit her chest.

She felt the knife under his pant leg with her bound hands, managed to grab the hilt between thumb and forefinger and pulled it to her chest above where his legs rested.

"Now get your damn legs off me," she gasped. "They're killing me. Turn around and I'll cut the line on your wrists. One-sided blade or two?"

He moved awkwardly but finally he was on his side, back to her, with wrists at her side.

"One-sided," he grunted. "Be careful. It's sharp."

She held her arms to her body with her hands grasping the knife's hilt. Using small body movements, she sawed the blade on the rope which tied his hands. Mackie worked by feel since there was very little light.

"Shit, that's me you just cut. No, don't stop. A little blood won't hurt me. You hold the blade still and let me move my hands against it. Yeah, that's better. I can feel it loosening." He rocked back and forth and positioned his body for a better angle at the knife. "That's it!" he said when the ties gave way and he could pull his hands apart. He faced her on his knees and swiped the blade between her wrists, freeing her.

"I owe you one, Agent Mackie." He put a hand gently on her head. "And I don't forget my debts." He looked around, felt his pockets, and cocked his head. "I still have my phone." He held it up. "I'm going to check the kayaks for our gear. You call this in. We're going to need some help." He started for the river, speaking over his shoulder. "You okay?"

"Just sore as hell," she said as she explored her chest with her now-freed fingers. "I'll survive." She looked up. "I guess I owe you one too, Michael."

"Yeah, yeah." He stopped, wiped his eyes and ran his fingers down his cheeks. "We should check inside. Sounds quiet."

"There's the woman who screamed," he whispered as they peered around the door jamb. "Don't even check. She's dead. Look at the head wound and the blood. No one could survive that." They continued to move through the house until Bent gestured with his thumb. "Outside."

They huddled on the front porch. "The professor's gone, and I'm back alone, Kate. I'm after these people while you deal with the office. My guess is they took him in the boat."

"What d'you mean, alone? We're a team," she hissed.

"We were a good team, Kate. But we now go our separate ways."

"No way!" she exclaimed in a whisper. "You wait for me at the kayaks. I'll call in and be right there."

"Kate, once you reach Perkins, he's going to order you to stand down. You have to follow his orders. I don't, especially if I don't hear them. Good luck."

She stood next to him. He put his arms around her in a light embrace and whispered in her ear, "Be careful. Things are sometimes not what they appear to be. Watch out for the white whale."

He headed toward the river, leaving her alone.

❧

Mackie's phone was not on her belt, so she walked to the corner where she had been shot. As she rounded the corner, she shuddered and reached for her chest. She knew she had to get over it. What did Bent mean?— *Look out for the white whale.* She searched the area where she had fallen, and, after a few minutes, found the phone and her pistol tossed in the brush a short distance from the house. She looked up gratefully as the moon emerged from the clouds. She holstered her gun and punched the numbers into her phone.

"We have problems, sir."

"What the hell do you mean?" Perkins responded in a threatening tone.

"Someone—actually a bunch of someones—were waiting for us at the house. I was shot, and Bent was knocked out—"

"Shot? What's your condition?"

"I think I'm okay. My vest saved me, but they tied us up and disappeared. We just got free, and Michael's off to follow them. We need help here. I'm going to join Michael, see if we can figure out where they went."

"Mackie, you just hold. You're going nowhere except back here. Stay on the line while I get some backup on the way. Just a minute while I make a call."

She waited. That's what the Israeli had said. That she'd be ordered to stand down. *Was Perkins the white whale?*

"Okay, Mackie, you there?"

"Yes, sir."

"There's a team on the way. They'll be there in ten minutes."

"The FBI?"

"Not exactly, Mackie. Better than the FBI on this stuff. Once they're there, you need to brief them. Then I need you back in Miami. Can you drive?"

"I'm pretty sore but I can drive. I think I should stay here, sir."

"That's a non-starter, Agent Mackie. We've had some developments, and we need to talk. Bent and the backup team can handle things there."

It was a direct order. She had no option.

"Well, unless Michael took it, our car's still at the marina."

"Agent Mackie," he yelled, "under no circumstances do you go close to that car!"

"I think I can drive, sir."

"Maybe you can drive. But not that car. I want the team to look at it. You remain outside and protect the crime scene till they get there."

Her phone buzzed as she disconnected with Perkins. "Michael," she said when she heard his voice.

"Kate, just want you to know our kayaks are still here. Looks like they left in that boat. Have you talked to Perkins?"

"Yeah. Just hung up. As you said, I've been ordered to do nothing but report back to Miami."

"Look, you've done your job. We found the guy. And I think I can find the boat. Tell Perkins I managed to put a GPS button on it before I was knocked out. Looks like they're heading downriver toward Fort Myers. Tell him I'll let him know when I find them."

"Michael, why doesn't Perkins want me to use our car at the marina? He ordered me to stay away from it. What's going on?"

There was silence on the line.

"Michael, you there?"

"Yeah, I'm here. Don't worry about the car, Kate. I might be a hard guy. But I pay my debts."

Kate couldn't just wait outside, not knowing for sure if the woman inside was dead. So she ignored Perkins's orders and went back in, moving slowly and cautiously this time. She carried her pistol in her right hand at her side, but she wasn't sure she'd be able to lift it if necessary. Her chest and shoulders still ached, with stabs of pain shooting down her arms.

As Michael had said, the woman lying on the floor in a pool of blood was dead, her face shattered. Going room to room more carefully this time, Mackie found the rest of the house empty. She returned her gun to its holster and returned to the front door.

Within minutes, she saw headlights coming down the approach road. The two sets were there too soon for them to be from Miami. They had to have been stationed close by. Two black SUVs pulled into the driveway and screeched to halts in front of her. Men exited each vehicle with drawn guns.

"Kathryn Mackie?" shouted the passenger from the first.

"Yeah, that's me," she answered. "I checked inside. They're gone. Left in a boat." She pointed toward the river.

The man approached her, lowering his pistol but not moving his eyes from her. "I'm told you've been shot. We'll try to help, but I need to see some ID."

Her eyes widened. "My ID's in my holster: a government-issued Glock. And my jacket says Secret Service. That's my only ID. Please cut the shit and get me some medical help. There's a body inside. She doesn't need any help. I'm sure Perkins told you I'm a black woman. Not too many of us hanging out on the Caloosahatchee at midnight on a Tuesday night."

"Yeah, you're right," he said as he holstered his weapon. "Sorry for the bullshit. John here's a medical technician. He'll take a look at you." Turning to the others, who had spread out in a small perimeter, he said, "Stan, try to help Agent Mackie." He pointed to another. "Reggie, check the back and down to the river. Bo and I'll go inside. Let's go."

After they confirmed the site was clear, the leader joined Mackie and the technician in the bedroom. "Stan says the vest saved you. You're lucky as hell, ma'am. I'm to get you back to Miami right away. Reggie's over at the marina checking your car. He'll bring it back and drive you—"

"I can drive," she interrupted.

He smiled for the first time. "Yeah, maybe you can. But you'll be going over a hundred miles an hour, and your arms aren't real strong after that shot. More important, we've been told to drive you."

Reggie came in and nodded to the man.

"Okay, we're all set. Why don't you just hunker down in the back seat and get some sleep. Reggie'll take good care of you." He offered his hand, which she shook gingerly. "Sorry about the way I braced you," he said. "Looks like you walked into a hell of a mess. We'll be here for a while, trying to figure it all out."

"I do have one question," Mackie said before he turned away.

"Shoot."

"Who the hell are you?" she asked with a grim smile. "I'm pretty sure you're not the FBI backup we had in place."

The man crossed his arms on his chest and shook his head. "You're right. We're not FBI. We take care of things the FBI won't touch. We clean things up after man-made disasters. But don't look for us in the Yellow Pages. Good luck, ma'am." He left the room.

Mackie turned to her driver. "Guess that's all I'm going to find out, right?"

"We're trained not to talk a lot, ma'am. But if you'll get in the car, I'll drive you to Miami as fast as I can."

CHAPTER 24
MIAMI DEBRIEFING

S he looked at her watch: two in the morning. She'd been cleared by the doctor, and Perkins was waiting to talk to her in the conference room.

"How do you feel, Kate?"

She shrugged. "The doctor says nothing's broken. Bruised ribs and chest contusions. No real damage." She sank into a chair. "Thanks for having the doctor here. Never been shot before. Didn't know what to expect."

"I know you're tired, so we'll make this short. I have a bunk available for you here so you can get some sleep. Our team's still at the house. You and I can go over everything in the morning. But we do need to know who these people were who attacked you."

"I wish I knew," she answered. "We were on the river when we heard a woman's scream. I beached and ran for the house with Michael somewhere behind me. I heard nothing more till my chest exploded. Afterwards, Michael said they couldn't have been private security; they wouldn't have attacked that way. Sorry, but other than that, I can't help." She paused. "One more thing. Michael called and told me he had planted a GPS device on their boat and it was heading for Fort Myers. He said he'd let you know when he found the boat. Maybe you should call him."

"We've tried," he said with raised hands. "He's gone silent. Can't reach him." He stood and directed her to the door. "Get some sleep. They've put some clothes and a toothbrush and essentials in the room for you. We'll talk first thing in the morning."

꙳

In the morning, Mackie was surprised that the entire team wasn't assembled. It was just the two of them again.

"How'd you sleep?"

"Like someone was jabbing knives in me every time I moved." She flashed a smile. "Other than that, like a baby. Where's the team?"

"If we've found the guy, we might not need the team. I'm waiting to hear from Bent. We do have some preliminary stuff from the house."

"Have you figured out who was there?"

"Not exactly, but we're pretty sure they weren't his friends."

"How'd you figure that?"

"The team found a thumb on the floor. It matches a lot of thumbprints in the house, so it's probably his. Fair amount of blood on the floor suggests it was cut off while he sat in a chair. And they found a body— a woman—dead in the same room. Shot twice in the head."

"Gold?" she queried.

"Not a sign of gold, no computer, no work papers of any kind. Someone cleaned the place out."

A knock sounded and a man entered. "Sorry, sir. It's important." He whispered a brief message into Perkins's ear. Perkins jerked up straight.

"Was it the boat?"

The man shrugged. "Too early to tell, sir. But it looks like it."

"Have them find out," snapped Perkins. "Real quick." He turned to Mackie. "About an hour ago, a boat exploded in the Fort Myers marina.

Big explosion. Looks like no survivors."

"Sir, Bent had Semtex in his kit. It had to be him."

"Yeah, you're probably right. He said he'd let me know when he found the boat. Just didn't expect the message to come this way." He stood and held Mackie with his eyes. "This certainly solves our problem, though, doesn't it?"

She looked back. "Was this the plan all along, sir? The reason Bent was here?"

"I never said that," he responded with a grim smile. "But it does take care of a lot of problems. Tell you what, Kate. Let's suspend till I know a bit more. You and I do have a few things to talk about, but first I'd like to know what happened with this explosion. You go home and get cleaned up. I'll get back to you by the end of the day."

"You're the boss, sir. But I do have one question."

"You always have one question, Agent Mackie. What's this one?"

"The car, sir. What was wrong with the car?"

He held his hands together, his lips pursed. "I guess that's a fair question. Bottom line is, there was nothing wrong with it, but there had been."

"What the hell does that mean?"

"The car had been rigged to explode, Mackie. But someone disconnected the trigger wire. Looks like someone changed their mind."

Or paid back a debt, she thought as she walked out of the room.

She was still deep in thought as she left the building and didn't notice the man approach.

"Agent Kathryn Mackie?" the suited man asked as he suddenly came alongside her.

She jolted alert and reached for her weapon. "Who wants to know?"

"You're in no danger, ma'am." With a sideways glance, he watched her hand on her piece. "I'm just delivering a message." He held out an envelope, which she instinctively took. He peeled off and disappeared.

She tore it open and found one piece of paper:

> *Kate. You are right to think something is amiss. Please go to the State Department consulate office where I have arranged a secure phone line. We must talk. Be discreet.*

There was no signature.

CHAPTER 25
RUNNING THE RIVER

The suspicions that Professor Conan had been taken away by boat were correct.

His hand had been wrapped with gauze and bandages they found in his bathroom. With a man on each arm, he was walked quickly to the boat tied at his dock. It was dark but he saw the boat silhouette sticking out beyond the dock, with outriggers and fishing rods pointing up into the night sky. It was big—at least forty feet, he thought. His right hand ached, and flashes of searing pain shot up his arm. Although in a daze, he managed to step into the boat before being pushed down a set of stairs to the cabin below. There he was thrown onto a cushioned bench in a corner.

"Stay here, señor, and be quiet. We will be in Fort Myers in less than an hour."

He closed his eyes, shaking uncontrollably, and curled up with his knees to his chest. He tried to elevate his right hand to stop the bleeding, but the bandages continued to ooze. He heard the men talking.

"Why not just kill him?"

"Because our orders are to bring him back alive, at all costs. Do not return without the professor. That's what they said."

"Why? Why do they want him?"

"They say he's a witch. He does some kind of magic. They want his magic to help the revolution."

"And Linda? We need to find her."

"I would like to," the voice answered, "but we're not going to find her. He either killed her or she ran. It's no longer our problem. We'll get his book in the morning and then head back. Others will have to worry about Linda."

The professor felt the boat move backward, swing to the left, and surge forward. He remained huddled in the corner against the cushions, thinking how his life had been shattered. If they were taking him to Cuba, it was over. He wasn't going to tell his secrets to the Cubans. His plan had been so good—make gold and make himself a hero but not destroy the world order. The Cubans would destroy everything if they learned his secrets.

He finally fell asleep with his hand on fire.

He woke to silence and a still-throbbing hand. But there were no engine vibrations. They were stopped somewhere. He had to pee.

"Señor, where do you think you're going?"

"I have to pee. Have to find the bathroom," he muttered.

"The bathroom is up top. Go take a piss off the bow. That is your bathroom," the man said with a laugh. "Don't fall off. There are sharks out there, and I see you're still dripping blood."

Conan stumbled up the stairs, using his left hand to steady himself on the rail while his right hung useless at his side. Once topside, he went around the cabin, followed the railing forward, and looked over the side into the black water.

"Shit," he said to himself. "I have to do it all left-handed. King of the universe, and now I'm peeing lefty and bleeding to death. A real fucking king…"

Bahoom!

He was flying through the air, his shirt smoldering from the heat of the exploding gases behind him. He smelled the pungent odor of burning hair—his hair. He tumbled wildly, hitting the water yards in front of the boat. He sank below the surface, swallowing and choking on water. Realizing he was under water, he stroked upward toward the surface, forgetting the pain in his right hand. On the surface, he breathed and swallowed gasoline-laced water. Flames flared all around him. He desperately swam away from the flames and reached a barnacle-encrusted piling, which he hugged, cutting his arms and cheek but welcoming the anchor to land.

He watched the shell of the boat he'd been on burn down to the water. Someone had blown it up. He knew that. He didn't know if they were after the Cubans or him. He only knew he had to get away.

He saw a ladder on the next pier. He swam to it and climbed, grabbing with his left hand and hooking his right elbow over the rungs. At the top, he rolled onto the boards and lay gasping. Light from the fire flickered all around him, but the sky remained dark. He heard sirens screaming and honking louder as they approached. On his knees, he pushed with his good hand and managed to stand and lurch toward shore. Where the hell was he?

"Sir, let me help you," yelled a man running down the pier. "Wait here and I'll get someone."

Conan focused on the Samaritan and raised his hands, one bandaged but now both bloodied. "Please, tell me where we are," he cried.

"Downtown Fort Myers, mister. The Fort Myers marina. Right off of 41. Someone's boat just blew up. Looks like you got burned in the

110

explosion. I'll get some help."

"Yeah, thanks," Conan answered. His mind was starting to come together. "I'll wait here. You get some help."

As the man raced away, Conan stumbled down the dock toward shore. He knew where he was, less than two miles from his storage locker. He had money there, gold, everything he needed. He had to go those two miles. He moved one foot after the other.

Just like one experiment after another. *That's it,* he thought. *I'm making gold. That took me ten years. This will be thirty minutes. One step after another. If I can do it, I can still make gold.*

The four-lane street cut through a seedy neighborhood. Small shops, junk car dealers, and pawn shops. He tried to walk quickly without running; running in this neighborhood would draw attention. He stepped back into the shadows every time he saw headlights, but the vehicles all sped by with sirens screaming. The exertion pumped blood to his hand, and he was soon leaving a trail of blood drops on the sidewalk. He fell twice, rolling to his left to break the fall with his left hand and then struggling up with one arm. Objects blurred as sweat dripped into his eyes, which mixed with blood as he tried to wipe it away.

He remembered his mother had always urged him on. *Don't ever quit, Henry. Work harder than the others.* He saw her face. She kept him going.

CHAPTER 26
FLEEING FORT MYERS

With his left hand, Conan couldn't get the combination. After racing along the deserted streets, ducking into the shadows to avoid detection, he had finally reached the storage facility. He figured out why he kept tripping when he looked down and saw the heels of his sandals burned and flapping loose. He wondered what the back of his shirt and pants looked like.

Panting from exhaustion and thirst, he jammed the lock against the fence with his bandaged right hand, closed his eyes as pain shot up his arm, and tried again. To the right past 0 to 1, back to the left to 9, right again past 6, then stopping at 6. Gold's atomic weight—196. He heard a faint click, and the lock opened. He was in.

"Imperial Cab."

"Yeah, I need a cab—need to be picked up."

"Where?"

"I'm at a convenience store on Palm Beach Boulevard, about a mile west of I-75."

"That's a tough area, mister."

Conan thought quickly. "Look, I need some help. I've been in an accident. My car won't run. I need to be picked up. I have money."

"Be out by the curb, not in the parking lot. We'll pick you up on the street."

"Oh, one thing."

"Yeah?" the voice asked with a suspicious tone.

"Tell the cabbie I look pretty bad. I'm all banged up from the accident. I'm carrying a black backpack, and…and my right hand is all bandaged. I really need a ride. Please hurry."

"Where to, mister?"

Someone was looking for him, maybe still trying to kill him. He had to get out of the area.

"South," he blurted. "Down to Bonita. I have a hotel room there."

CHAPTER 27
A WAKE-UP CALL

"Hello," Mackie said groggily into the phone after it woke her.

"Mackie, it's Perkins. I need you in here right away. We have a problem."

"What—what's going on? What's the problem?"

"I can't get into it on the phone," he shouted, bringing her fully awake. "How soon can you get here?"

"Give me an hour."

"Bring an overnight. You're going back to the West Coast. See you in an hour."

John Perkins dialed the number with trepidation. It was answered after two rings.

"Yes?"

"John Perkins again, sir."

"I know who the hell it is. But why again?"

"A complication, sir."

"I don't like complications."

"I know, sir. I don't either." He paused, met silence, and continued. "It now looks like he's still alive."

"You've got to be shitting me, John."

"Wish I were, sir. We found a receipt for a commercial storage place in his house. Went there and found it empty."

"So what?"

"We got the security video from the storage company. They show a man going into the locker a little after seven this morning. Blurry image but the right body size. Left after a few minutes with a bulging backpack. And the guy's right hand was bandaged up, held close to his side. We think it was the professor, sir."

"When was the explosion?"

"A little after five, sir."

"I don't like this, John. It was supposed to be all wrapped up."

"I know. I have Mackie coming in. I'm going to send her after him."

"She's not Ishmael."

"No, she's not. And I'm not, either. We cannot do what he could do."

"Well, what can you do, John?"

"I don't know yet. I'm working on it."

"There's a lot at stake. Can you control Mackie?"

"Yes, sir. I can control her."

"Agent Mackie, you look a bit more rested. How's your, uh…chest?"

She smiled. Her breasts hurt like hell, but she'd be damned if she'd tell him that. "I'm still sore but I'll survive. Someday I would like to thank whoever makes those protective vests." She leaned on his desk. "What's the problem?"

He gestured for her to sit, drummed his fingers for a moment, then blurted, "I think the professor survived the explosion."

Mackie straightened and stared at him. "That's a problem?"

He tried to stay calm as he looked at her. "Let's say it's an unexpected development," he answered. "We have him on a videotape accessing his storage locker this morning, a couple of hours after the explosion."

"And?"

"He disappeared with a backpack filled with whatever he took out of the locker."

"So why don't you just have Bent chase him down? He's your pet assassin, isn't he?" Her eyes were steady on his.

Perkins sighed. "Bent's gone. He probably was responsible for the explosion, and he probably thinks Professor Conan is dead. His kind doesn't stick around."

"I'm not an assassin, Perkins, so why am I here?"

He stood and paced, eyeing her. "I know you're not an assassin, Mackie. And you're not being asked to be one. But we still have to find this guy and make sure he doesn't bring down our financial system. You're the best available."

"Yeah, since he didn't kill me either, right? I was supposed to go down, wasn't I?"

He stopped pacing and stared at her. "God damn it, no, Mackie. I would never permit that. I didn't know about the car bomb, but after he took off, I did get suspicious." He froze with hands trembling at his sides. "It was me who warned you not to take the car! I would never let one of our people get hurt. I don't work that way." He paused for a moment. "Look, I know you called your old friend President Menton, and I know you talked a bit out of school with your friend in Washington."

"And how exactly do you know that, Mr. Perkins?" she said coldly.

"This isn't kindergarten, Mackie. We tapped all your phones and emails. It's standard practice with high-security teams. You all signed waivers."

"So you think I'm a snitch. Why the hell am I still here?"

"Because I think you can help. Right now. Today. And I don't think you'll snitch again."

"Why's that?"

"We've dealt with President Menton. She thinks you're just in a tough assignment with me…and that I'm a real asshole."

Mackie's eyebrows peaked, a small smile on her lips. "Fine, but I'm not sure I want to work for an asshole, John."

"I can't force you to. But you know this guy has to be caught. Remember, he killed a girl. If you won't help, we'll have to get someone else. You can go back to chasing bad money. That'll be the extent of your career."

"That's all I had anyway."

"No. You once had—and wanted—more. And your friend Jonathon up in Washington now has a security asterisk on his record which will haunt him for his entire career."

"You are a bastard, Perkins."

"I'll take that as a compliment." His hand formed a pistol with forefinger extended. "I want you in Fort Myers, and I want you to find Professor Conan." His eyes, cold and hard, focused on hers then glanced away. "And I promise, we're not going to kill him. You've won that one. We're going to rain on his parade and ruin his grand plan, but he'll live. Beyond stopping him, I don't know what we'll do with him. We turn him over to the state, they'll prosecute, and he'll probably get the death penalty. He has a bargaining chip, and he'll use it. He goes public, we have a worldwide financial catastrophe. So I'm still working on our next step. But you gotta get this guy."

She knew she had a role to play. She had to go along with this asshole, at least for a while. "The Israelis are not going to be happy when they learn he survived," she suggested. "Will they send Michael back?"

"If they learn." He held out a newspaper. "Look at the headline—*No survivors in marina explosion.* We're going to keep the professor's survival very, very quiet. To answer your question, I don't think we'll see any more of Michael Bent. No matter what, they never send the same guy a second time."

"You're not giving me much of a choice." She stood and placed both hands on his desk, her face only inches from his. "But who am I working for? You're not with the Department of Justice, and as far as I know, this entire operation is unauthorized and illegal as hell. I'm not going down and maybe going to jail for you."

He didn't flinch or move back. "This operation is authorized at the highest levels, Agent Mackie. Higher than you can imagine. And I am assigned to Justice for its duration. That's all I'm authorized to tell you."

"How about my friend? Will the asterisk disappear?"

"It'll be gone by tonight."

"Okay, I'm off to Fort Myers. Not for you, and not for the ones at the highest levels. The son of a bitch killed that girl in the Everglades. He has to pay for that."

Within an hour, Mackie was back on I-75, driving west. Perkins said others were working on the explosion and the storage site and running down leads on a disheveled man who was seen leaving the marina. Her phone buzzed. She pulled it to her ear.

"Mackie here."

"Perkins here. I'm with Ceshire. He's picked up an interesting story."

"Yeah?"

"About an hour ago, Israel announced that it had uncovered a large gold seam in a Dead Sea Scroll cave near Qumran. It said it hopes to now be able to mine its own gold. As I think you know, Mackie, prior to today, there were no known gold deposits in Israel."

"And you think our friend reported the professor dead this morning, right, sir?"

"I'm sure he did."

"And in less than a day, Israel announces that it has a legitimate way to produce gold," Mackie said. "Pretty coincidental, I'd say."

"Damn coincidental, Agent Mackie."

"Don't think the Israelis are going to be very happy when they learn he survived," she added.

"If they learn, Mackie. If they learn. We're going to keep the professor's survival quiet. Who knows?" Perkins said in a tone reflecting thought. "If they can find gold in an old cave, maybe we can find some too. We have a lot of abandoned mines out west, some on federal land. This guy might be worth more alive than dead.

"We also have a lead for you. There's a cab company, Imperial Cab, that picked up a guy near the storage site early this morning."

"Where'd they take him?" she asked.

"Don't know yet. They're running down the driver. Want you to interview him as soon as they find him. We'll probably know before you get there. We'll call you."

CHAPTER 28
THE CABBIE

She met the cabbie at his dispatch office in a dingy strip mall on Route 41. Mackie was sitting in her car when he pulled in, having been called in by the dispatcher. She jumped out before the driver went inside.

"Mr. Blain?"

"Yeah, that's me." He hunched his way to her car, short and nondescript, just another guy.

"I asked your office to call you in, sir." She pulled out her photo ID and showed it to him. "I'm Special Agent Kathryn Mackie with the Department of Justice. Need to ask you some questions."

He glanced at her ID. "You don't have to tell me. It's about my first fare this morning, isn't it? I knew there was something wrong about the guy." He backed up, his face showing alarm. "Am I in some sort of trouble?"

"No, sir. Not at all. But you're right about the fare." She looked at a pad she held. "I think you picked someone up at the convenience store on Palm Beach Boulevard, a little after seven? That's who we're interested in."

"What'd he do? Rob a bank?"

"No, he didn't rob a bank. Don't you worry about that. We just need to know where you took him."

"That's easy." He pointed over his shoulder with his thumb. "South, about fifteen miles, to the Trianon Hotel in Bonita. That's where I dropped him. Pretty odd duck. All beat up and bandaged."

"What do you mean?"

"Well, he said he'd been in a car accident. Clothes were soaked like he'd come out of the river, smelled of gasoline, and his right hand was bandaged. When he got out of the car, I saw his shirt and pants were burned in the back. He swore me to secrecy, said he didn't want his family to know where he'd been." He shuffled his feet. "You're the feds, right? So what did he do? Kill a guy?"

"I can't get into that, Mr. Blain." She shrugged. "Sorry. Did you see any weapons?"

"No way," he exclaimed. "I wouldn't have picked him up if he had a gun. All he had was a black backpack. He was a sorry-looking dude."

"Okay, Mr. Blain. You've been a big help. If we need anything else, we'll call you." She held up both hands. "But, please, this has to stay confidential. It's more than sworn to secrecy. It's a federal investigation. You talk to anyone about this, it could be obstruction of justice." Her eyes held his. "Understood?"

"Yes, ma'am. My lips are sealed."

Mackie turned to leave, but he raised a hand for her to wait. "Agent…?"

"Mackie," she answered. "Kathryn Mackie."

"Yeah, Agent Mackie. One more thing. Don't really want my boss to find this out."

"What, sir?"

"At the hotel, the guy gave me five hundred to go out and buy him some clothes and first-aid stuff. For his hand, he said. I got the stuff and left it at the front desk for him. Only cost a little over a hundred bucks, so I kept the rest. Put down another fare to cover the time. Do I have to give that back? You know, stolen money or something?"

Mackie smiled. "No, Mr. Blain, you keep the money. It wasn't stolen. Thanks for your help."

Agent Mackie got back in her car, leaned against the headrest and thought for a moment. She knew she should call Perkins, but she also now knew she couldn't trust him. He'd tell her to wait for him or some other type of backup, just as he had delayed them from getting to the professor's house earlier. She should have been there before last night. The attackers, whoever they were, probably wouldn't have been there; the other woman wouldn't have been killed; and Conan wouldn't have escaped. This Professor Conan wasn't a dangerous guy—probably unarmed and on the run. If she didn't move quickly, he'd run right away from her.

She entered the Trianon Hotel into her GPS and drove south with an estimated time of arrival of twenty minutes. She was sure she could handle him.

She stopped in front of the lobby at eight o'clock. The man at the desk looked over her identification and confirmed that a Mr. Henry David was in room 302. He hadn't checked out yet and had paid cash. After some back-and-forth, he handed her a pass card. She assured him there would be no scene; he was just a missing witness for a federal trial. She was going to serve him with a subpoena and wait around to make sure he appeared in court in the morning.

Mackie knew the lock would beep or click when she inserted the card, so she knelt on one knee and pushed into the door with her shoulder as it unlocked, staying on her knee as the door swung open.

"Who the hell are you?" yelled the man on the bed. He was on top of the covers and bolted upright as she pointed her Glock at him from her kneeling position inside the doorway.

"I'm the law, Professor Conan. United States Justice Department. You stay right where you are, or I'll shoot you dead."

He froze, eyes bulging. She saw white bandages on his right hand and bottles and tubes on the night table. Bloodstained bandages made a disgusting pile on the floor. He wore jeans and a sweatshirt and was barefoot. A two-day stubble of black beard made him look wild and disheveled.

"I'm going to make sure you don't have a weapon, Professor. Then I'm going to handcuff you." She stood and stared at him while pointing the weapon. "Are you going to give me any trouble?"

He trembled, tears streaming down his face. "No, I won't give you any trouble," he said in a shaky voice. "Are you really the police? You're sure you're not with the Cubans? Please, don't hurt me anymore," he sobbed.

"I'm the police, and you're not going to get hurt if you cooperate. Don't know what you mean about Cubans. You just stay right on that bed and put your hands behind you."

She approached him slowly, checked for weapons, then clipped his hands behind his back with a plastic cuff.

"My hand," he cried. "Be careful. They cut off my thumb. I think I'm going to lose my hand. It's all red and inflamed. I need a doctor."

"Everything okay in here?" came a voice from the doorway.

Mackie turned and saw the desk clerk peeking around the jamb.

"Yeah, we're fine," she said over her shoulder as she turned back to her prisoner. "I served the papers, and we're all set. I'll be calling in some more help so I can go home. Please close the door."

Once the door closed, she pulled out her phone. "It's Mackie. I have him cuffed and under control.... The Trianon Hotel in Bonita Springs, right off of Route 41.... Sorry, couldn't wait. Had to move quickly. I'll explain it when you get here. I assume you're coming?.... Good. We'll wait. Room 302. Looks like he needs a doctor for his hand.... Yeah. Missing a thumb—probably the one found in his living room. He's saying something about the Cubans."

She hadn't taken her eyes off Conan while she talked. He remained seated on the bed.

"We're going to have about an hour's wait, Professor. Some assistance is coming, and hopefully they'll bring a doctor." She pointed to the corner. "I want you to move to that chair."

He did so but winced when he sat and leaned back. "Can you put my hands in front? I can't lean back with them behind me. My hand's killing me."

"I think you're just going to have to sit straight till help gets here. I want your hands to stay behind you. And although I have a lot of questions for you, we're going to wait for the others."

He closed his eyes. "You promise it's not the Cubans?" he pleaded.

"There are no Cubans coming, Conan. We're all from the good old U.S. of A. And now we're just going to be quiet till the others get here."

"Sir, it's Perkins. We've got him.... He's under restraint at a hotel in Bonita Springs. Mackie's with him. I'm on my way. I'll be there in less than an hour.... I have a plan, but I'm going to need some help. It's a little unusual, but I think it solves our problem—not only solves the problem but turns it into a huge success...."

CHAPTER 29
TURNING THE SCREW

In a little more than an hour, there was a knock on the door.

"Agent Mackie, Perkins."

She opened the door and saw he was accompanied by two other men. She recognized them from the night before: Perkins's clean-up crew.

"These guys are from the house team. They met me outside." He made no attempt to introduce them. Striding into the room, he made his way to Professor Conan, hands on his hips. "So you're the guy who's given us so much trouble, huh?"

Conan sat shriveled in the chair and looked up with fear in his eyes. He didn't speak.

Perkins spun toward Mackie. "Look, you and I need to talk for a few minutes. These guys"—he indicated the two men in the doorway—"can watch him. Let's go outside." Once the two of them had walked down the hall, he said with a grim smile, "I'm going to turn the son of a bitch," he whispered.

"What do you mean, turn him?" Mackie asked.

"He likes to make gold, right?"

"Y-yeah," she answered with hesitation.

"We're going to give him the opportunity to make gold, but not for himself—for us."

"What the hell are you talking about? He killed a woman!"

"I'm going to deal with that," he said, waving his hand. "I want to go back in there and have you follow my lead. I'm going to beat up on him a little, and you're going to play nice. I'll do the talking. You just give him some motherly love. He'll come around."

"John—"

"Look, Mackie, we have a deal, remember? Don't you go backing out on me. What I'm doing is fully authorized, again, at the highest level."

"And when am I going to find out what that means, sir?"

"Soon enough. Right now I want to get to this guy while he's down, and he looks like he's pretty close to the bottom. Let's head in. Just follow my lead."

She had a role to play, so she did as he directed, following Perkins into the hotel room.

ॐ

"You are Professor Henry David Conan, right, sir?" Perkins had taken up his place in front of the shackled man, hands on his hips.

"Yes. That's me." Conan looked up at the man, unsure what to think of him.

"I'm with the Department of Justice. We've been investigating a conspiracy to distribute counterfeit gold. We believe you're behind the conspiracy."

Mackie tugged his arm and whispered something in his ear that Conan didn't catch.

Perkins wheeled and pulled her away. "Just shut the fuck up," he hissed. "He'll get his rights." Turning back to Conan, he continued, "Agent

Mackie thinks maybe I should give you your rights, mister. Well, let me tell you what your rights are. You can remain silent and refuse to talk, and I'll then hand you over to the state for the crime of murder. You'll wait in a state jail or prison till convicted, but I don't think it'll get that far. Those guys who cut off your thumb last night—Cubans, weren't they?—those guys are all over the state jails here. I think you'll lose the other thumb in the first week. And your balls after that. And you certainly won't live till trial. Now, mister, those are your rights. Should we continue our conversation?"

Conan had pushed back in the chair, ignoring the pain from his hand tied behind him. "I—I didn't say I wouldn't talk. But I didn't do those things. I just need protection from the people who are chasing me. I need help with my hand."

"Oh, yeah, the hand." Perkins turned to one of the other men and held his hand out. He was given a small cooler. He turned and dropped it into Conan's lap.

"There's your thumb, Professor. All nicely packed in ice." He paced back and forth, staring down at the cooler. "I have a hand surgeon ready to fly down here tomorrow and reattach your thumb…if you cooperate with us. If not, the thumb's still yours, and you can carry it over to that state jail I mentioned."

Conan was fuzzy but not completely out of it. He was terrified. He glanced over at the backpack full of gold and research notes… and the journal. They had him on the gold, but no way they had him on Linda.

"I'll cooperate," he screamed. "Yeah, I've done some stuff with gold. I'll tell you everything. But I don't know anything about a murder. A murdered girl? I haven't killed anyone."

Perkins looked over at Mackie, nodding to her that it was her turn. She took the cue.

She knelt beside Conan's chair, placing a hand gently on his left arm.

"Professor, we'll help; we will. We'll fix your hand. We'll protect you from these people who are chasing you. But we know you killed the girl. You have to tell us everything."

"There's no evidence," he cried, almost pleading. "No evidence I killed anyone!"

"Cut the shit, Conan," Perkins jumped in. He pointed at one of the other men. "This man's a forensic specialist. He found a chair in your house with traces of duct tape on the arms—same duct tape found on the corpse. The corpse you dumped out in the swamp." He swung around. "You know what else he found? He found stains on that chair's seat. He thinks it's urine. And blood on the floor. We don't have the results yet, but I bet she peed in her pants while you tortured her. If the DNA from those stains matches the corpse, you're a dead man. And who knows who killed the woman we found in your house? Maybe they'll charge you with her death also."

The professor knew all was lost. They knew about the gold and about Linda. He gulped and swallowed hard. "If you know all that, why aren't you just calling the police and putting me in jail? What do you want from me?"

"We want you to show us how to make gold, Professor," Perkins said. "You're out of the business and in deep shit. We're thinking of going into the business. And we might be able to clean up your shit."

Professor Conan was in no position to bargain. He pretty much agreed to do whatever they wanted if they'd fix his hand and protect him.

Perkins didn't let up on the pressure. "Remember, Conan, you're as good as convicted of murder. Your life is changing real fast…and changing completely. Don't think it's going to be back to life as usual. You're going to do time—with us rather than on death row—and afterwards, you might go back to teaching, but you'll have nothing to do with gold. Once you teach us your system, you're going to forget everything. And to make sure you do, I'm going to have a videographer here in the morning."

"W-what do you mean?" he stammered.

"I mean we're going to make a movie, Professor. And you're going to be the star. You're going to answer every one of our questions…on camera. If you fuck with us later, if you misbehave at all, that film will go to the authorities, and maybe, just for good measure, to the Cubans."

Conan closed his eyes. Tears streamed down his cheeks. He couldn't even wipe them away with his hands cuffed behind his back. "Gold's my life, my soul. I can't live without gold. I'm the first who's been able to make it. You're taking away my life."

"God damn it, Conan! You took it away yourself when you killed this woman and tried to become master of the universe."

Mackie spoke up. "Professor, it's been a long day. You know you have to cooperate, but I know it's hard. We'll deal with it all in the morning." She turned to Perkins. "Can we clean up his hand some?"

"Yeah," he murmured, pointing at one of the other men. "Stan's a medical technician. He has a kit outside. He'll clean it up." His hands went to his hips. "But that'll be it unless you're fully on board in the morning. I'll make arrangements for the surgery tomorrow night. It'll take place only if you do the video. Mackie, come with me," he directed as he left the room.

Perkins led Mackie outside to a platform overlooking the river that flowed behind the hotel. Looking around to make sure they were alone, he faced her with hands in his pockets. "Thanks for the help in there," he said quietly. "And good job catching the son of a bitch." He paused. "I need you for the video in the morning. He likes you; you calm him down. After that, I'll get his hand done, and I'm making some plans for a place to set up shop to make gold."

"You're serious about that?"

"Damn right. And I'll need your help with that, too. Gotta keep him calm and happy if he's going to do us any good. But look, after the video session, it'll take me a few days to get things organized. You do the video in the morning, and then take a few days off. You deserve it. Go take that vacation we made you cancel."

"Yeah, I almost forgot. You heard my phone calls, didn't you?"

He pulled his hands out of his pockets and shrugged. "Just doing my job. See you in the morning."

A few minutes later, Mackie was walking to her car when her phone buzzed. Holding it up to the light, she saw it was Jonathon.

"Jonathon, what a nice surprise. Where are you?"

"I'm in Miami, sitting in front of your apartment, waiting for you to come home."

"You're what?"

"I'm in Miami. Decided you might need some help. So here I am."

"Oh, Jon, I'm so glad to hear your voice, and I could use some moral support, but I'm across the state in Bonita Springs."

"Where's that?"

"Right next to Naples, just over two hours from Miami if you do the speed limit. But I'm supposed to be at a meeting here at eight in the morning. I was just heading off to find a room."

"Fine. Find a room and I'll join you. Just let me know where."

She had kept walking as they talked, and now she paused outside her car. She'd been shot, almost blown up, and was now conspiring to break the law. She needed a friend. But she wasn't ready for romance. Not now, not tonight.

"Jonathon, it's been a tough couple of days. I want to see you, have you hold me. But I'm too beat up right now for much more. Can you understand?"

"Sure. I'm here to help. No foolin' around is what you're saying. You let me know where. I'll be there."

"Thanks, Jon. But guess what?"

"What?"

"After tomorrow's meeting, I have a couple of days off. Maybe we can have our little vacation then?"

"I'm here for whatever you need."

Her eyes widened as she remembered her calls were being monitored. "Just come and hold me tonight. I don't want to talk about anything. I can't talk about anything."

"I'm on my way. Call me with directions."

"I will. Just get on I-75 and head for Naples. I'll call as soon as I find a room." She hung up. "But not on this phone," she murmured to herself. "I'm not going to let that son of a bitch listen to any more of my calls."

A quick search on her phone showed a Hyatt just a few miles south. She drove directly to the hotel. It was early summer, so they should have rooms, she realized, and they did. She checked in and hurried to the fifth-floor room so she could call Jonathon. Looking at her watch, she figured he'd still be on Alligator Alley, halfway across the state.

"That you?" he answered.

"Sure is. I'm at a Hyatt, just ten minutes west of the highway."

"I was starting to wonder if you'd changed your mind."

"Not at all." She let out a deep sigh. "It's a long story, but I didn't want to use my cell. I'm in room 505. Left a key in your name at the desk. Told them to ask you to show identification. Hope you don't mind. Have you had dinner?"

"Nope. Was planning to take a good-looking girl out to dinner in Miami. Places open late around there?"

"I doubt it." She laughed. "The old people live over here. They're all in bed by now. I don't have the energy anyway. We'll do room service, if that's okay?"

"Sure. Give me the directions, and I should be there in half an hour."

Mackie cleaned up and was dozing on the bed when she heard a soft knock and click at the door. Opening her eyes, she saw Jonathon juggling a bunch of flowers and a small overnight bag. She stood, and they hugged.

"Oh, Jonathon, the flowers are beautiful. You're such a romantic." Holding him tight, she sobbed quietly. "It's been tough. Last night they shot me and tried to blow me up, and now I'm sort of a spy for President Menton. I just don't know what to do. You're the first one I've been able to talk to—"

"Shot you?" He pulled back and looked at her. "What d'you mean? What happened? Are you okay?"

She grinned through her tears. "Yeah, I'm okay. My vest stopped the bullet, but my chest is sore as hell. And I did catch the guy we've been looking for."

He kissed her lightly and held her again.

"Not too tight." She winced. "I'm still sore."

He took her by the hand to a cushioned chair and helped her sit. "You sit and relax. Tell me all about it, and we'll figure things out. I have some of your favorite pinot grigio—not sure it's still cold. We'll just use the plastic glasses. I even remembered a corkscrew." He held it up with a flourish.

As she told her tale, he interrupted occasionally with astonishment and reassurances. They finished the wine and decided to skip dinner.

"Will you just hold me, Jonathon?" she said. "Hold me so I can sleep. I've been running on nervous energy. I think for the first time, I've been scared and I couldn't show it. I'm on stage again in the morning. I need to sleep."

He pulled her close under the covers. "You get some rest. In the morning, we'll talk about what you do next."

"I do what I have to," she murmured as her eyes fluttered shut. "I do what I have to…"

CHAPTER 30
REPORTING BACK

When she woke, Mackie used the hotel phone to call the number she'd been given.

"This is Mackie," she said when her call was answered. "I'm sorry, ma'am, but I haven't been able to get to a better phone.... This is the hotel phone where I stayed last night. No one knows I'm here. I'm pretty sure it's a safe line.... The Hyatt in Naples.... Yes, back across the state. Look, this is important, ma'am. I got him. His name is Henry David Conan—*Professor* Henry David Conan. He's the goldmaker. I found him last night holed up in a hotel in Bonita Springs. Now Perkins has come up with some crazy scheme for him to teach us how to make gold.... 'Us' is the United States, or at least that's what Perkins says. I'm supposed to participate in some type of video interrogation of the guy in the morning. They say we're going to hold him and make him show us his secrets.... I still don't know who's in charge. All he says is, 'at the highest level.'... I know, I know. I have to find out.

"Do I have to do this interview? I feel sort of like a spy, or a traitor.... I trust you, ma'am, but it is me all alone down here doing this.... Well, I hope there are some others on our side out there. I sure haven't seen them…. I'll stay as long as I can. He told me I could have a few days off after this interview while he gets things set up, whatever that means…. I should be able to call again in the afternoon, after the video…. I know. I won't use my cell phone…. Thank you. Good-bye, Madam President."

❦

Back at the Trianon, at about the same time, Perkins placed another call to his boss.

"Yes, Mr. Perkins?"

"We're ready for this video interview. I've got a video operator. Were you able to line up an office?"

"Yes. A small law firm in Naples. Bork & Mugby, on Seventh Avenue. They have a conference room available all day. They think it's a medical malpractice case. They'll be very discreet. Mugby is the contact, if you need one. But probably won't be necessary for you to talk to anyone. Just go in, do the job, and leave. I'll have someone there to pick up the tape afterward. You don't need to retain a copy."

"Yes, sir. Any luck on a holding facility?"

"I think I've come up with a perfect solution, Perkins. There's a medium-security prison nearby that the state just closed. Too old and expensive to operate. I'm trying to work out a lease for a year or so to conduct some highly proprietary and confidential fish farming, using solar rays to heat the water. How's that sound?"

"Sounds perfect, sir. Keeps him in and the bad guys out." He paused. "Are there any bad guys still out there, sir?"

"You know, I'm not sure on that one. The Cubans have their tails between their legs, and the Israelis think he's dead. But we have to protect him. I've seen pictures of this place. It's tight. Double concertina razor wire fences and in the middle of nowhere. No one's going to get in there unless we want them to."

"What is the place, sir?"

"Hendry Correctional Institution, built in 1977. East of Naples in the middle of the fucking Everglades. I don't think anyone ever escaped from it, or at least escaped and survived the alligators." He laughed. "I think it'll be a perfect place for our Professor Conan."

CHAPTER 31
MAKING A MOVIE

"Professor Conan, are you giving this statement of your own free will and without any pressure or duress?" Agent Mackie read from the script. She waited for the whole farce to implode when the professor explained how he had been forced to this room and coerced into cooperating. She was in a conference room at a Naples law firm to which she had been directed when she phoned in. A video camera purred at the end of the table, and a stenographer typed on his machine.

Perkins had met her in the hall before she entered the room and handed her a sheaf of pages with scripted questions. "Just read the questions to him in a pleasant tone. Don't sound tough or overbearing. Don't worry. He'll cooperate."

Conan was seated and looking down when she entered the room. He raised his head and looked at her. She took in his clean-shaven face and new shirt. He'd been cleaned up. But his eyes were glazed and unfocused, as if he were in a trance.

"Yes, ma'am. This is a free and voluntary statement," he said in a barely audible voice. His eyes shifted down to the table.

She stared at him, tipped her head in amazement, and took a deep breath. She continued the questions.

"Have any threats been made to you, sir, or have you been promised anything in return for your statement?" Looking for his bandaged thumb, she knew that would blow it up. But the thumb wasn't visible. Both of his hands were under the table in his lap, not visible to the camera.

"I have received no threats, and nothing has been promised."

Looks like the answers, as well as the questions, have been scripted, she thought. Guess I'd better just read the questions.

"Do you know you have a right to a lawyer and a right to remain silent and say nothing?"

He nodded toward her. "I want this all off my chest, Agent Mackie. I waive those rights, and I want to answer all your questions."

"Directing your attention to the night of May fifteenth, sir, ten days ago. What happened that night between you and your student, Linda Chavez?"

This gave him pause. Beads of sweat popped on his forehead, and for a second she thought he was going to wipe them away with his mangled right hand. Not so. He raised his left hand. Then she saw why. *Jesus Christ.* His right hand was tied to his leg under the table. He couldn't raise it if he wanted to.

He swallowed and answered, "I invited her to my house and gave her a dose of the drug GHB. After she was unconscious, I raped her." The sweat was running down his cheeks. "I then put her body into my golf cart and drove about a mile into the Everglades across from my house and left her body there." His head was hanging and his words barely audible.

The stenographer interrupted. "Sir, you'll have to speak up, and please look at the camera."

He jerked up and stared at the camera with wide eyes. "I raped her and killed her. Is that good enough?"

"Thank you, sir."

Mackie continued. "Was Linda Chavez dead when you left her in the Everglades, Professor Conan?"

He stared at her. "No, she wasn't dead. But she was unconscious. I wouldn't have left her out there conscious."

"Why not, sir?" she asked, off the script, as she thought his gratuitous comment had been.

"Because I didn't want her to feel it when the animals came, God damn it! I was trying to protect her from the pain."

Mackie took a deep breath, not sure she could continue without attacking him. She closed her eyes, tried not to think of the woman, and forced herself to the next question. "How was it that a gold nugget was found on her body, sir?"

He was breathing deeply. "I gave it to her to get her to come to my house. Told her I had more at the house. I lured her with the gold."

There were another dozen questions, about Chavez being tied up, peeing on the chair, how and where he had taped her. But there was nothing about the Cubans, nothing more about gold, nothing about events two nights ago. He was admitting to rape and murder. But nothing else.

After the last question, Mackie left the room. Perkins stood outside, an earpiece in his ear.

"Okay, Mr. Perkins, I'm done, and now I'm going to get a shower and try to wash off all the shit that was in that room."

"Good job, Mackie. I heard it all. You did a great job. It had to be done. Take the rest of the week off, but call me Monday morning." He tried to pat her on the shoulder, but she ducked and slipped by.

"Just a second, Kate," he said, holding up an envelope. "Here's a bit of a bonus to help on your vacation."

She took the envelope, surprised that it was heavy. "What is it?" she asked.

"One of the gold coins from his knapsack. Three or four ounces. He won't need it, and you earned it. You can cash it in at any of these gold shops—"

She interrupted him. "You want me to take evidence as a personal *bonus?* Now you wouldn't be trying to set me up, John, would you?" She handed the envelope back. "You keep it. I don't want the professor's gold." She pointed her finger at him. "You are going to keep your promise, right? You're going to fix his hand?"

He slid the envelope into a pocket and nodded. "It's all set. The doctor's flying in tonight to sew his thumb back on." He swiveled his head to make sure no one was within earshot, then continued in a low voice. "We'll talk Monday. We're not finished with the professor yet. You might not want his gold, Mackie, but he is going to teach us how to make it. Now go get some R and R."

"Mr. Perkins," exclaimed the hand surgeon after he had examined Professor Conan. "What the hell happened to him?" They were standing in the reception area of an outpatient surgical center not far from the Trianon Hotel. It was ten o'clock at night.

"I told you, Doctor, he lost his thumb."

"He didn't lose that thumb, sir." He gestured over his shoulder to the examining room where he had left the professor. "Someone hacked it off, and there's a raging infection in his hand." He shook his head. "It's also been a while since it happened, hasn't it?"

"Only about forty-eight hours," Perkins said. "Look, can you sew it on?"

The doctor stared at Perkins, rubbed his forehead, and sighed. "Of course I can sew it on. But the thumb joint's shattered, and I don't carry replacement joints in my travel bag." He waved his arms, indicating his surroundings. "This place looks pretty good, but it's not a hospital. He needs a continuous IV drip for the infection, and I'd like time to stage a real surgical procedure. Otherwise, he's not going to have much movement in that thumb."

Perkins shook his head. "Look, Doc, this guy's not a friend. He's a scumbag drug dealer who got hurt when he cheated a customer. He has some intelligence value to us, so I promised we'd sew the thumb back on if he cooperated." He stuck out his hand and flicked his thumb. "I didn't promise he'd be able to flip a coin with it. Just sew the damn thing on. That's all we promised."

"I have to tell him what I can do and what I can't do," said the doctor.

"Go ahead," snapped Perkins. "Tell him what you want. But it has to be done now—tonight. Otherwise we'll just give him his thumb, and he can do whatever he wants with it."

CHAPTER 32
A ROMANTIC WEEKEND

When Mackie got back to the Hyatt, Jonathon was sitting in the lobby. He had already checked out. They had agreed she would not call. No way was she going to use her cell phone. His raised eyebrows sent a silent question as she walked to his chair. He hugged her gently.

"How'd it go?" he whispered in her ear.

She raised her hands, and shrugged. "If you mean, did I violate his rights and probably break the law, it went great. I made my first movie, but I don't think too many are going to see it." She shook her head. "It was pretty bad. He admitted to raping and killing the girl, and now we've hired him to show us how to make gold. The whole thing is sick."

"Kate, you're not breaking the law. You're trying to catch whoever is."

She nodded. "Yeah, you're right. But I don't have to feel good about it."

"So now you have some time off?"

She smiled. "Yep, that's the only good part. I'm off till Monday, and"— she placed her arm through his—"there's a guy I owe a vacation to. Where are we going?"

"The Florida Keys," he answered. "I've found a place in Islamorada that has a tiki hut on the beach. This time of year, they're not full, so I reserved it. Only about a three-hour drive."

"That sounds great, Jonathon. Let's just leave my car and my cell right here in the garage and take yours. I don't trust these guys. If they can tap my phone, they can probably trace it. And who knows about the car? I don't want them knowing where I am." She leaned up to his ear. "I don't have many clothes," she whispered.

He put his arm around her as they headed to the door, whispering back, "You won't need many."

The Islander was a large motel complex on the Atlantic side of Islamorada, about seventy-five miles south of Miami. By driving the old Tamiami Trail, they were able to completely avoid Miami's congestion. On Islamorada Key, the motel had been around for many years, but the owners had updated the units along the water to resemble beach tiki huts with amenities. In the middle of the complex a large saltwater pool beckoned, and that became their first destination after they checked in and Kate bought a bathing suit in the gift shop. They lay drying in the late-afternoon sun after their swim.

"I now feel clean," Kate said. "It's a different world. Oh, darn! I was supposed to call President Menton."

"We can call from the room," answered Jonathon. "No one's tapped this line. They don't know where we are."

She made the call on the room phone. "Ma'am, sorry I'm late calling.... Things went pretty much as planned. I did the video, in which he confessed to raping and murdering the girl, but there was nothing about making gold or Cubans or anything else.... No. It was all scripted. I was given the questions and told to read them.... No one but Perkins, ma'am. Still don't know who's running the show.... I'm off till Monday. I'm supposed to call him Monday morning about the gold.... I'm at this number through the weekend. Hopefully on vacation.… Yes, ma'am. I'll call once I know more."

She hung up and looked over at Jonathon. "Sorry. I think that's it. What's that?"

He was holding up a bottle of wine in one hand and a pair of glasses in the other.

"Oh, you found some wine? And real wine glasses this time?" She stood and embraced him with a deep kiss. "I think we should get our wet suits off," she murmured in his ear.

"Here, I'll help."

She winced as he brushed her chest. "That's my sore breast. Be gentle."

"Sorry," he said and moved to provide attention to other parts of her body.

She moaned softly. "Feels better already. Oh, that's not my breast. But it feels good, too. Let me love you, too. Let's just forget everything and love each other."

They did just that until Mackie rolled off him and lay panting on the bed. "Jonathon, I need to come up for air." She reached over and stroked his chest. "How about dinner? Should we do something about it?"

He leaned over and kissed her bruised breast. "After that dessert, I'm not sure I'm hungry."

She laughed and pulled his chest hairs. "I said dinner. Not more dessert." She pushed him away. "I think you should take me out for dinner." She stroked him gently. "Then we'll see about more dessert."

They woke early and decided to run on the beach. He was faster but didn't have her stamina. After a mile, she caught up and ran smoothly at his side while he sucked air. Sandpipers scurried in and out with the waves in front of them, always leaving a safe space between themselves and the human intruders. Alongside glided a flock of pelicans, skimming the water's surface in search of breakfast.

"I think you have to withdraw," he gasped, looking over to see her reaction.

"I've thought about it," she answered, breathing easily, "but I do have President Menton counting on me. If I bail out, they're going to get away with all this."

"Kate, she's no longer the president." He paused to suck some more air. "She really has no power or authority. You could be left out there swinging when everyone starts running for cover."

She caught his eyes then quickly turned away. "There is one other thing." She ran for a few more strides. "They're sort of blackmailing me."

"What?" he yelled, grabbing her arm and pulling her up short. "What do you mean 'sort of' blackmailing you?"

"Let's sit," she answered, pulling him to the sand. She put a hand to her mouth in thought. "If I don't play along, I'll never get back to presidential protection."

"That's not a disaster, is it?"

"Maybe not. But there's something else." She paused. "It involves you."

"Me? What the hell do they know about me?"

"Remember the tapped phone calls I told you about?"

"Yeah." He stared intently at her.

"Well, they heard you talk about your contact at Justice, your friend who gave you some information."

"Okay," he said slowly.

She leaned back on the sand and looked up to the sky, avoiding his eyes. "If I don't cooperate, they say you'll lose your security clearance…for a long time."

"Those bastards!" he exploded. "That explains a couple of things."

"What do you mean?"

He moved over to look down at her face. "I've tried to call that friend a couple of times since. He won't return my calls. And I was summoned into the managing partner's office last week."

"What happened?"

"That's just it. Nothing happened. When I got there, he said there had been a mistake. That he'd gotten notice that my clearance was under review. But a few hours later, he was called and told a computer malfunction had caused the message and that everything was fine."

She moved her eyes to his. "I'm not going to ruin your career, Jonathon."

He nodded. "And I'm not going to let you get hurt, either."

She stood and pulled him close. "So what do we do?"

"I'm not going to let you do this alone, Kate. I'm going to help."

She turned and kissed him. "You know, I really love you."

They had two more days to enjoy together before Monday morning arrived.

Monday morning they departed early, hoping to reach the Naples area by nine. The sun was rising slowly out of the dark Atlantic on their right, and as they drove over the bridges, shadows danced way out into the Gulf to their left. By the time they reached the Everglades, the sun was directly behind them. They talked about Jonathon's helping, and they finally agreed that he could do more good back in Washington than in Florida.

"Look into the Israeli angle, Jon. The gold they've suddenly discovered. It's too coincidental that they sent Michael Bent—an assassin—and then announced the find right after he reported Professor Conan was dead. And I'm going to let President Menton know you're involved."

"She's not going to be happy about that." He swung out to pass a pickup.

"You're probably right. But I'm getting a little tired of making everyone happy. I'm the one with my neck out here, and I'm going to start protecting it."

"I knew you had some spunk." He chuckled and punched her lightly on the shoulder as he pulled back into the right lane. "Did I tell you I enjoyed the weekend?"

"No, I don't think you did," she said, smiling and patting his leg. "Now what exactly was it you enjoyed?"

He grabbed her hand and squeezed it. "I enjoyed you, Kate. Every inch of you. And when we get through this, I want to enjoy you for a long time, a real long time."

"That would be nice." She straightened in her seat, clasped her hands to her face, and shook herself back to the present. "Now I have to call this asshole and check in. Could I use your phone?"

"Go right ahead. Give him my best."

She punched in the number with a grim look on her face. "Mr. Perkins, this is—"

"Mackie! Where the hell have you been?"

"I've been on vacation, sir, remember?"

"When I said vacation, I didn't mean drop off the face of the earth! I've been trying to reach you."

"What's so important, sir?"

"Your boy Conan is what's so important. He's evidently taken a liking to you. He wants to talk to you, and only to you, about the gold. You should have heard him when he was under anesthesia. Kept saying we're all evil…except for Agent Mackie. In his eyes, you're on a fucking pedestal. And if you're interested, he thinks you have good teeth, whatever the hell that means."

"Well, I'll be in Naples in about an hour. Where should I meet you?"

"The same hotel. It was easier to stay here than move, and the surgical center was just down the street. We'll be relocating tomorrow. I'll tell you all about it when you get here." He remained silent for a moment, as if unsure. "Anyone with you?"

"That, Mr. Perkins, is none of your business. What I do on my time is my business."

"Just don't forget our deal, Mackie."

"I'm sure you won't let me," she shot back.

CHAPTER 33
THE GOLD TEAM

At the Hyatt, Jonathon drove to where her car was parked, and they sat in his car for a few moments.

"I hate to leave you down here with these guys, Kate."

She leaned over and hugged him. "I'll be okay. You've made me stronger. I'm going to get this thing done." Holding his face with her hands, she kissed him. "You know why? Once it's done, we can be together again." She slid out of the car, wiping a tear away before he could see it. "Let me know what you find out about the Israeli gold, and by then, who knows? I might be able to tell you how to make American gold."

She waved as he drove away. In her car, she turned on her cell phone and saw a number of messages. Most were from Perkins, which she deleted. But two were from her supervisor at the Secret Service, which she decided to return.

"Bob, Kate Mackie."

"My gosh, the long-lost Agent Mackie. How are you?"

"I'm up to my ears in this special assignment you gave me, and when this is over, you're going to owe me big time."

"Tough one, huh?"

"You got that right. Wish I could tell you more, but you know it's hush-hush. I think you've called me a couple of times. Long story, but my phone's been off. What's up?"

"Just trying to pass along a family message, Kate. Your mother called here a couple of times looking for you—"

"Did you say my *mother*, Bob?"

"Yeah. You have to keep in touch with your family."

"Bob," she said slowly, "my mother's been dead for four years. You sure it was my mother?"

"That's what she said. I don't know what's going on."

"What'd you tell her?"

"Nothing, really. Just that you were on a special assignment and we'd try to get a message to you."

"Shit. That told her I was still out on this assignment. That's what they were trying to find out. When were the calls?"

"Let me look here. I think I have the slips. Yeah, here they are. Friday. She called twice on Friday."

And Conan was supposedly killed Wednesday morning, she thought. Someone was checking to see if I was back with the Service, off the special assignment.

"Is there a problem, Kate?"

"Might be. Might be. If you get any other calls about me, please try to trace them, and let me know. And, Bob?"

"Yes."

"My father's dead, too. I have no mother or father, nor do I have any brothers or sisters."

"I'm sorry about that."

"Yeah, me too. I guess I'm pretty much all alone. But I have to go to work. Say hi to the team. I'll be back one of these days."

She was worried. If someone was looking for her—and she thought she knew who—they might not have bought the story. They might not be convinced the professor was dead. That meant she might be doing more than learning how to make gold; she might be protecting the son of a bitch.

Perkins was sitting in the lobby of the Trianon Hotel when she walked in. He waved her over.

"Welcome back, Agent Mackie. You all relaxed and ready to go?"

She nodded with a wry smile. "I'm fine, Mr. Perkins. I guess I need you to tell me exactly where I'm going. What's next with this guy?"

"Fair enough." He pointed to the seat next to his and leaned in her direction so they could talk quietly. "I've made arrangements for you and the professor to set up shop close by to restart his work. The team has disassembled everything at his house that we think he'll need, and it can be put back together at the new site. As I said on the phone, he's not being real cooperative with us, but he's real anxious to see you. You did something to bond with the guy. I have no idea what, but it makes you an important part of the program."

"How'd the surgery go?"

"Fine. The doctor says he might not have good movement, but it's back on. Still bandaged up, but he'll have a thumb."

Mackie clasped her hands in her lap and leaned in. "John, there is one thing."

"Yeah?"

"I need some reassurance that I'm not going to go to jail over this."

"What do you mean? I've told you we're fully authorized."

"Sure, you've told me that. But I know people have been indicted for lesser things, and some of them were in government and thought they were authorized. I need to get it from the source, John. I need to talk to whoever is authorizing me to do all this."

He gazed at her and stroked his chin before answering. "I understand what you're saying. I'll make some calls. Let me try to get you a call this afternoon which should satisfy you."

"I need to make the call, John."

"Why's that?"

She stood and pointed a finger. "I want to place a call to a known government office—and it better be a high one—and I want to ask for the person I'm going to talk to. That's my requirement, and it's not negotiable. No matter what deal we had and what you threaten."

"And if I can pull that off, Mackie? Are you then fully aboard?"

She nodded with resignation. "Yeah, then I'm fully aboard. I'm on the team…with Professor Conan." She twisted a ring on her right hand. "I guess the professor and I will be the gold team. That's what you can call us: the gold team."

⁂

"Department of Justice," said the soft voice that answered her call.

"Yes, this is Special Agent Kathryn Mackie of the Secret Service. I believe Attorney General Abbot is expecting my call."

"Please hold while I put you through, ma'am."

"Attorney General Abbot's office," said the next voice—a male this time.

"Hello. This is Special Agent Mackie—"

"Yes, ma'am. The attorney general is expecting your call. Just a moment."

"Special Agent Mackie, this is Howard Abbot. I'm glad to talk with you. I understand you've done great work and captured this guy who was causing so much trouble."

"Yes, sir. I captured Professor Conan, and I understand I'm now under orders to work with him on his gold-making project."

"Well, um…um…you certainly get right to the point, don't you, Agent Mackie?"

"I imagine your time's pretty valuable, sir. I just want some reassurance that what I'm being ordered to do is legal and fully authorized."

"I'm not sure ordered is the right word."

"Oh, yes, sir. I want it clear that you and Mr. Perkins are ordering me to do this. I'll do it and I'll do it to the best of my ability, but it's not my usual line of work."

"Okay, Mackie, you just do what Perkins asks you to do. He's working for me. That enough for you?"

"Yes, sir. Thanks for taking—" He had hung up.

She was now on the gold team.

Professor Conan was pacing when she entered his hotel room, and he looked more put-together than when she'd last seen him. There was a bulky bandage on his right hand with tubes running to a small pack hanging from his shoulder. She recognized it as a cooling pack for the swelling. He spun as she entered.

"Agent Mackie!" He welcomed her like a long-lost friend. "I was starting to wonder if you'd ever get here."

"I'm here, Professor. Guess we're going to work together on this gold thing. How's the hand?"

He held it up. "It throbs, but they say it'll be okay. On Thursday the doctor's coming back to check the stitches. Have to wear this cooling pack till then." He smiled at her. "I'm so glad you're here. Now we can work together."

She stood where she was and stared at him. "We are going to work together, Professor, but we're also going to have an understanding."

"An understanding?"

"You're a killer, Professor Conan. You killed that woman in the

Everglades."

He put down the left hand he had extended and shrank back.

"Looks like you got away with it. And now you and I are going to work together to make gold. But don't for a moment think we're friends or associates or anything like that. I'm as much your jailer as your assistant."

"I thought we could be friends," he whispered as he hung his head.

"You thought wrong."

CHAPTER 34
HENDRY CORRECTIONAL INSTITUTION

The plan was to drive the professor to the prison Thursday night after his stitches were taken out. Mackie and Perkins made the trip on Wednesday to pick locations for a lab and living quarters. Mackie also wanted to check security. She hadn't told Perkins about the calls from her dead mother or her suspicions that someone was still pursuing their captive. Conan had said he'd need southern exposure for the towers with the parabolic mirrors and a nearby supply of clean, running water. All his equipment and belongings had been trucked down to the prison. It was only about an hour and a half from his house.

"It's certainly isolated," Mackie noted as they drove through the open, barbed-wire gates. "And huge—much bigger than we really need."

"Yeah, we'll just use a small area," Perkins responded as he drove. "Can't be too picky when you're looking for a secluded, open site." He grinned. "And not that many jails on the market. Once there were eleven hundred prisoners and a couple hundred guards here. Now we'll have one detainee and just a few guards."

"What about the university? His job?"

"Took care of it. Had the doctor call to advise the university he was badly injured in the home invasion; it did get some press, you know. We put it out as a bungled robbery. Told them he'd been med-evaced north for treatment and rehabilitation. They put him on an indefinite leave." He laughed. "Those academics will believe anything. They'll even continue his pay. Just hire someone else and take tuition up a percent or two."

"It's going to be tough for just a few of us to secure this place." She appraised her surroundings. "What is it, about a half-mile-square?"

"Don't worry. No one's going to try to get in. We're not even going to lock him in a cell. Put a monitor on his leg, and he won't go anywhere."

"Hope you're right, John. Have you figured out who the Cubans were at his house?"

"No, we're still working on that."

"What about the woman he killed in the marsh, and the one in his house?"

He turned, not grinning this time. "Always another question, isn't there, Mackie?" He pursed his lips. "The authorities still have the one from the marsh as Jane Doe. We're not telling them anything else. The lady in the house was a bartender from a place across the river. Don't know why she was there or who killed her." He pulled to the building on their left and cut the engine. "Don't worry about the Cubans or the dead ladies. They're history."

"A jail? You told me if I cooperated, I wouldn't go to jail," Conan yelled two days later when they told him their destination. He and Mackie sat in the back seat as Perkins drove.

"Calm down," Mackie answered, patting his leg. "It's a closed jail, which we've rented to make sure we can keep you safe. You won't be locked up in a cell or anything like that. It's a perfect location for your work—in the middle of the Everglades, with plenty of sun and open space for your mirrors."

"What about water?"

"We're going to build you a river," she explained. "Our cover story is we're farming catfish and using a new, proprietary process to heat the water with sunlight. Speeds up the growth cycle of the fish. So we bring in a backhoe and dig down a foot, and we have water. A lot cleaner than the Caloosahatchee."

"Are you staying there?" he asked.

"I'll have a bunk available, Professor, and I'll stay on occasion. But remember, I'm not the one who killed that girl. I'm not the one who's in trouble. There'll always be someone there to protect you."

"Do I still need protection?"

"There were a lot of people interested in you. We can't guarantee some aren't still out there. That's why we found this place. Not to keep you in…to keep everyone else out."

Conan's eyes bulged. "They're still after me?"

"No, no. This is only a precaution, Professor. We don't think anyone's going to bother you. Take a look." As they turned onto the approach road, they could see the facility. "It's very secure."

The sign, bordered with rolls of razor-edged concertina barbed wire, read, Hendry Correctional Institution. The gate under the sign rolled open as their three vehicles approached. A large, dark hulk rose like a ship above the cleared marshes of the Everglades.

"You're home, Professor," barked Perkins from behind the wheel. "This is home till you teach us your tricks." He turned in his seat. "All of them, right, Professor?"

Conan sighed and nodded.

Once their convoy drove inside, the gate rolled shut, and they proceeded to a building on the south side of the center prison yard.

As they exited the car, Conan grabbed Mackie's arm. "Can I explain something to you, Agent Mackie?" He nodded toward the others, who were going inside. "Privately?"

She shrugged. "Make it quick."

"You know what I said the other morning about the girl—Linda?"

"Sure. You raped her and killed her. I heard it loud and clear," she hissed and started to follow the others.

"Agent, please. I never raped her. Perkins told me I had to say that." He took a deep breath. "I killed her, yes, but I would never rape anyone."

Mackie stopped and turned. "Well, then, what the hell do you say really happened?"

"Linda was some sort of a Cuban agent. She seduced me about a week before and drugged me. While I was unconscious, she searched my house and stole my secrets about making gold. I killed her to defend myself, to protect my secrets. I didn't know what else to do. Then the Cubans came and attacked me and tried to take me back to Cuba." He grabbed her hand. "Agent Mackie, you have to believe me. I would never rape a woman. I couldn't do that."

"And you claim Perkins knows all this, including the young lady and the attackers being Cubans?"

"Yes, ma'am. He knows everything."

She bent close to his face. "You sure about that?"

"That morning, before you came in with the questions, I told him everything. I swear."

She stood straight and looked over her shoulders to where the others had gone. "Okay, I've heard what you said. Let's go in. We'll see how things go. For now, nothing changes."

CHAPTER 35

A TALK WITH THE EX-PRESIDENT

After settling Conan into his new quarters in one of the prison's open-bay housing units, Mackie got a ride back to Naples. She might have a bunk available, but she was damned if she was going to sleep at that place unless absolutely necessary. And she had a call to make on her new, disposable phone, which was probably not traceable. At least, she thought not. Her room was at the downtown Marriott.

"Hello?" answered Ms. Menton.

"Ma'am, it's Mackie."

"Yes, Kate. All moved in?"

"He's there. Wasn't real happy when he learned it's a jail, but I quieted him down. I'm back at my hotel on my new phone."

"I've heard from your friend Jonathon. Seems like the level-headed type. If you trust him, I guess I'll have to also."

"With my life, ma'am."

"That's good enough for me. He's told me about your Israel theory. It's intriguing."

"I have something else now, too."

"What?"

"Professor Conan pulled me aside and said he never raped the girl, that she was a Cuban, and that the Cubans who invaded his house were looking for her as well as his gold. Says they were trying to take him to Cuba."

"And I imagine he now says he didn't kill her, either? That she just wandered off into the Everglades?"

"No, that's the interesting thing. He still admits he killed her. Says he did it to protect his secrets, that she was some type of agent. And what I find most interesting, he says he told Perkins all this, and Perkins insisted on the rape story and on keeping the Cubans out of the video."

"Well, well," Menton said slowly. "It is a mess, isn't it? And it looks like an international mess. With our government right in the middle."

"So what do I do now, ma'am? Can we bring them down now?"

"Unfortunately, not yet. I'm sure this goes beyond the attorney general. We have him cold with your phone call, but we have to get them all or they'll climb back in their holes. The country needs you, Kate." There was a short silence. "On the Cuban thing, I think I'll call our old friend Hassie Chamoun. I think she's still in Miami. If anyone can find out what they're doing, she can. After all, he's her father. She certainly established that with those documents she released last year. Will you stay on, at least till I get some feedback from her?"

"I guess I do still owe you one, ma'am."

"No, Kate. Not as a favor to me. It's more important than that."

"I haven't quit yet."

Hassie Chamoun, she thought. *I saved her life twice. Maybe she can help me now.*

CHAPTER 36
RECONSTRUCTING THE WORKSHOP

It took two weeks of hard work to build another workshop for Professor Conan. They had to break out a south-facing wall and insert a large window to collect the solar rays. Two of the parabolic mirrors from his house were mounted on the existing guard towers at the corners of the prison walls and linked to the motorized guidance system he had developed. At the same time, a backhoe was brought in to dig a pond. A pump and pipes brought the water to the new window. Conan insisted that the PVC pipes first delivered be replaced by clay. "It all has to be natural," he insisted. "Plastic is not natural."

"This is the easy stuff," the professor explained to Mackie. "Once the mechanics are set, the real work starts. Anyone can melt lead and add small amounts of gold, but transmutation requires much more. The principles of the Emerald Tablet, as translated in Newton's journal and perfected by me, rely on the power of the sun and the moon and the natural earthly forces below. Remember always, the sun is the father of all matter, and the moon, the mother. I must fertilize the lead with moon rays and then transform it with the sun. Everything requires timing and precise measurements. It took me years of experiments to perfect the process."

Perkins was nearby and listening. "I assume anyone can make the gold once the process is understood, Professor?"

Conan turned to him. "I cannot guarantee that. Alchemy is as much a religion—an appreciation of the forces of nature—as a chemical process. I dedicated my life to its principles and was successful. I believe in the principles." He raised his hands as a question. "Whether a nonbeliever—a heathen, if you will—can do the same, I don't know."

"Well, we're going to find out, aren't we?"

"Yes, we will find out."

"And in order for you to get out of this place, the answer better be yes, mister."

"I understand, Mr. Perkins."

At the end of the first week, an express package was waiting for Mackie at her hotel. She scanned it at the desk and saw it was from Jonathon. In her room, she found a handwritten note at the top of the first page:

> *Kate, this might be more than you wanted, but it's what I could develop on the Israeli gold.*

A typed memo followed:

> *The Israeli find of gold in a Dead Sea cave has been trumpeted as a major geological find, although the exact location has not been identified and a number of questions have been raised. The authorities in Israel are claiming this to be the long-lost gold mine of King Solomon from three thousand years ago—when he built the First Temple in Jerusalem. Up till now, it was thought the mine was in Egypt or Africa. It was called Ophir in the Bible, and it has never been found. At least, not found and identified as the biblical Ophir gold mine.*

The Israelis claim this mine will generate thousands of ounces. That would put it near the top of producing gold mines.

The Dead Sea caves are located in an arid desert area. There's plenty of sunlight, which you explained is necessary for the process, but very little water.

I decided to play around with Google Earth to see what I could find in the area. It's where the Sadducee sect's ministers hid their manuscripts in the first and second centuries, still largely wild and undeveloped. The area has been aerially mapped by Google, but I encountered an unusual void in the maps.

In an area in the mountains near Qumran, there's no mapping. A superimposed legend says, "Not available for viewing at this time." I contacted Google to get an explanation but got nowhere.

So I started doing a little detective work. From the adjoining Google maps, I identified the closest roads and structures and, with a little more effort, placed some phone calls. I became an official of the Israeli Road Department investigating traffic patterns and learned there's been a dramatic increase in traffic over the last six months into the blacked-out area. Over the last sixty days, a big water tanker drives to the site every day. So there's your water.

This find is more than just some new gold. If it's as big as they say, it could be a game changer in the Middle East. Israel would have much more financial self-sufficiency and maybe need less aid from us. The Arabs would love us to cut aid to Israel, but they don't want the Jews to have strong financial resources. So I don't know which way it cuts.

She read it twice. She now understood why Bent wanted to eliminate the professor. She imagined he wouldn't stop till he knew he had. There was too much at stake. She sent Jonathon an email:

Thanks for the message. Please share it with our friend.

CHAPTER 37
BEING WATCHED

The next day, Professor Conan announced he was ready to prepare for the first melt. He and Mackie were standing at the new window, arranging the mold of lead and a small beaker of gold shavings.

"I prepared the lead during the last full moon, back at my house," he explained as he positioned it on the spot he had marked on the sill. "They brought it down with the other stuff from my lab."

Mackie bent down to watch closely when a glint hit her eye from the tree line two hundred yards away. Her Secret Service training took over, and she quickly pulled the professor away from the window.

"Just a second, Professor. Thought I saw something over there." She pointed to the trees. "Probably nothing, but I'd like to check it out before we keep standing in the window."

"Oh my God! Are they coming for me again?"

"No, no. I'm sure it's okay. Can we do the pour tomorrow?"

"Yeah, but I have to reprogram for sun movement and maybe prepare some more lead. Let me check on tonight's moon—maybe there's enough remaining."

"Well, is that going to be a problem?"

"No, I guess not. I'll work it out." He looked over to her. "What are you going to do?"

"Right now I want that compass of yours. I want an azimuth to the point where something flashed. In the morning, I'm going over there to take a reverse reading and find the spot."

"You're going to stand in the window?" he said with a shaky voice, handing her the compass.

"Don't worry, Professor. If there's anyone there, it's not me they're looking for." She slid over and looked down at the compass, which she held below the window on the workbench. *At least, I hope not,* she said to herself, holding her breath. "One hundred eighty degrees," she murmured. "Due south from this window."

"What do we tell Perkins?"

Releasing her breath when nothing hit her, she said, "Just tell him it's too cloudy. The guy's no alchemist. He'll believe you."

That night she slept in her cot at the prison for the first time. She wanted to be out in the field early in the morning, at sunrise.

She slipped through the door at the southwest guard tower at six, having gotten a key from one of the guards. She told the guard she'd be going outside the walls.

"I'm doing a perimeter walk," she explained. "Just to make sure there are no surprises out there."

She followed a dirt road south toward the tree line. She wanted to make noise to scare off any animals, but she knew she couldn't. Instead she moved quietly. In twenty minutes she was at the trees, and the sun was starting to brighten the surroundings. She heard some slithering and small chirping noises in the grass but hadn't stepped on anything—not yet, anyway. She turned right and walked along the trees, looking down at her compass. In about a hundred yards, she thought she was at the right spot.

She stood still, turning her head from side to side and up into the low trees. *Would I pick this spot? No sun in my eyes, straight across to the window, about the closest spot with concealment.* Something ran through the brush behind her. It was small and low to the ground—nothing to worry about. She felt dampness in her armpits, and decided to sit and wait for a while. As she sat, her hand landed on something unnatural. It crackled, and her hand slid a few inches. It was still too dark to see the ground, so she used her flashlight. Cupping the beam to keep it concentrated and small, she pointed it to the ground.

She was looking at sunflower hulls—empty, discarded sunflower hulls. She shivered and looked around again. Michael Bent had been here, watching them, chewing his sunflower seeds and spitting out the hulls.

The question was, had he been watching them through binoculars or a gun sight?

She imagined he had been carrying both. A swishing sound and motion from above pushed her into a roll as she grabbed for her pistol. The large cat hit the ground six feet behind her and raced into the woods. She didn't even have the pistol up before it disappeared, but she saw a long, swinging tail. That meant a panther. Most people never saw the elusive panther. This one must have been right above her head, watching her, on the same perch Michael Bent had used.

She walked slowly back to the prison gate, not bothering to stay along the tree line.

"Find anything, Mackie?" asked the guard inside.

"Saw a panther. Think he decided I was too big to eat, so he ran away."

"Yeah, it's panther country," the man replied. "Used to hunt them when I was a kid, but no longer. Not many left." He pushed the gate open for her to enter. "Anything else?"

"There's a place out at the edge of the trees where someone's been." She shrugged. "Don't know when, but we're doing some experiments this afternoon we don't want anyone to see. Maybe you could have someone do a few patrols this afternoon…along the tree line?"

"I can put someone out there for the entire afternoon if you want."

"No, that's probably not necessary. Just have some activity out there." She didn't want Bent to know he'd been detected. She just wanted to keep him away for the afternoon.

"And if you don't mind, I'm going to keep the gate key in case I have to go out again."

"No problem," he answered.

CHAPTER 38

THE GOLD TEAM

At one o'clock, the three of them were in the new workshop.

"You ready today, Professor?" asked Perkins. "Not too many clouds?"

"We're set to melt in…" he looked down at his watch, "thirty minutes. We should have gold by four."

"I'm going to be real interested in seeing this," Perkins said. "Still think this alchemy stuff is a bunch of mumbo jumbo."

"Well, sir," spoke Conan with hesitation, "that's part of the reason I think you shouldn't be in here when I perform the transmutation."

"What the hell you talking about? Of course I'm going to be here. That's the deal. You're teaching us to make gold."

Professor Conan stood with hands clasped. He grimaced. Mackie noticed that, as usual, his right thumb was tucked under. It still carried a small bandage.

"Mr. Perkins, this is not just turning on a switch. It's alchemy, one of the earliest attempts by civilized man to understand and impact the world order. It's older than most religions." He separated and spread his hands.

"It is a religion."

"I don't care what you call it, Conan. I want to see how it works."

"That's the point, sir. If you're here, I fear it won't work. You'll contaminate the process with your negativity and…with…you! You're anathema to alchemy."

"And what about Mackie? You want to keep her out, too, so you can do everything in private—no witnesses?"

"I've thought a lot about that. I think she'll be okay. She has a heart; you don't. She listens; you yell. I think she can love, but you only hate. I think her essence is compatible."

"Well, I'll be goddamned, Mackie," he said. "Sounds like you're a real pushover." He walked over and leaned into her space. "You two been talking about this…about how you're the big lover?"

Mackie narrowed her eyes. "No, John, not a word. It's the first I've heard anything about it."

"Well," he said, "what d'you think?"

"I have no idea. My job is to protect Professor Conan and assist when asked. So if he were to ask me to stay out, I'd stay out. I don't really give a damn what you do."

Perkins backed up and glared at them. "You got your wish, Professor." He spun and growled over his shoulder, "I'm out of here, but I'll be right outside. I expect to see some gold by four." He slammed the door.

Mackie took a deep breath and turned to Conan. "As he said, you got your wish, Professor. Now tell me what to do."

Conan walked to the workbench and pulled over a container of lead. From a small safe underneath, he withdrew a bowl of gold shavings and talked to Mackie while working. "First, we have to weigh the lead and the old gold. I say old gold only to differentiate from what we will be making. They will end up being identical—or almost so—but you must only add old gold to the lead to make the new gold."

"Why's that, Professor?" she asked, walking to the bench and looking over his shoulder.

Almost muttering as he slid over an electronic scale, he said, "Because although I will transform the combined metals to gold, the atomic weight of the new gold will be slightly higher than that of old gold. Probably because lead's atomic weight is higher. It's a technical point, but in my early experiments, I tried to use the new gold to make more new gold and always failed." He turned to her. "I think you're aware that I had a weight problem with some of the gold?"

"Oh, yeah. That's how I got dragged into this in the first place," she answered with raised eyebrows. "If you'd done it better, neither of us would be here. And I would have preferred that."

"Not as much as me, Agent Mackie." He glanced down at his scarred thumb. "I think I solved the weight problem in the pour I conducted for…" He grimaced and closed his eyes. "For Linda Chavez. The nugget I gave her was almost perfect."

Mackie nodded. "You're right. We weighed the nugget we found on her body and found it closer to the correct weight than the earlier gold. But it was still slightly off."

He backed away from the bench. "What about Linda? Does it make any difference to you that I didn't rape her?" He looked like a sad puppy seeking reassurance.

"I'm not your judge, Professor. It makes no difference what I think."

"It does to me," he said softly, still pleading for forgiveness.

"I am not going to forgive you, Professor. Sure, the killing is more understandable as you've explained it. But still not forgivable." She pointed at the bench. "Now let's get back to work. We have a time window, don't we?"

"Yes." He looked at the clock to the left of the window. "In twelve minutes, the mirrors will focus solar rays on the lead. It will melt at about 620 degrees, but then it has to go up to almost two thousand degrees to melt the gold. We'll then add the old gold. In some way, and I'm not exactly sure how, some of the lead protons are then destroyed and transmute to the lower number of gold protons. It all becomes gold, but it has to be quickly cooled in fresh, running water."

"Sounds too simple, Professor."

"Once you figure something out, that's what they always say."

She stood back and watched. An hour later, he dunked a mold of molten metal into a trough hanging outside the window. Water flowed through the trough.

"About five minutes," he said.

"It didn't work!" he cried. He was looking down at a mold containing a grayish metal block.

Mackie, standing shoulder-to-shoulder with him, viewed the same thing. "What the hell happened, Professor?"

"I don't know," was his panicky response. "I did everything the same as before. It always worked before. Dozens of times." He put hands to his face and looked at her. "What are we going to tell Perkins?"

She returned his gaze. "The question is, what are you going to tell him? This isn't my show." She turned toward the door. "Might as well bring him in now. There's nothing for him to contaminate."

She opened the door and waved Perkins in, commenting as he walked by, "There's a problem."

He strode to the bench and stared down at the blob of metal. "What's the problem?"

"It didn't work, Mr. Perkins. I did everything as before, but it didn't work. Maybe the different location or water, but I can't explain it."

John Perkins stood rock still for a moment. Then he pulled up Professor

Conan's right hand, causing the man to wince in pain.

"I fixed your fucking thumb, Professor. I saved you from the Cubans. I built this place to your specifications. Don't tell me you can't explain it." He bent, almost spitting in Conan's face. "You're fucking with me, Professor. You sent me out so you could screw this thing up, and I'm not sure that Agent Mackie cares one way or the other." He pointed over his shoulder toward Mackie. "You're going to do this again tomorrow, and I'm going to be in here. My technical people have reviewed your notes, and you're going to take us through this step by step. If you can't make gold, you're no goddamn use to me. Maybe I won't rip the thumb back off, but I'll sure as hell turn over you and the video to the authorities. You'll be a dead man, Professor."

When Perkins let go of his hand, Conan shrank back at each yell. "I'll try, Mr. Perkins; I'll really try. I tried today. I'm telling you the truth when I say I don't know what happened. Ask Mackie."

"Hey, guys, don't bring me into this argument. I have no idea how to make gold. I just watched what he did." She walked out, adding, "I'll be back in the morning." She stopped at the doorway, pivoted, and looked at Perkins. "Unless you don't want me here, sir?"

Perkins stared back. "No, you should be here, Mackie. Don't want him to have some other excuse, like he needed your loving presence to help the process." He turned back and nodded at Conan. "Even though it didn't do a hell of a lot of good today."

CHAPTER 39
THEY ALL RETURN

Mackie stormed out, jumped into her car, and sped west along the two-lane Route 858, better known as Oil Well Road. The son of a bitch Perkins had as much as accused her of complicity with Conan. She screeched into the left turn toward I-75 to get back to Naples. She was so distracted, she didn't see the white panel truck pull out behind her from the convenience store on the corner, nor the gray Honda, which pulled out behind the truck. She wanted to be home by five; she knew she had to make some calls. This assignment was ending.

When she got home, she dialed a number on her cell phone. It went straight to voice mail. "Ma'am, this is Mackie. The professor was unsuccessful in his experiment today. He'll try again tomorrow. Once you get this message, please do what's necessary to get me out of here. Conan's hitting on me, Perkins just about hit me, and I've found we're being watched by the Israeli. I've taken it just about as far as I can. I need some help down here." She hung up and dialed again.

"Jonathon, I'm home after an unsuccessful day at the office.... Yeah, it failed. I was with him during the whole process. He explained it all, and it sounded like something out of a science-fiction magazine. And that's the way it turned out. He ended up with the same glob of lead he started with.... I don't know what went wrong. He says he doesn't know. Naturally, our friend Perkins blames me.... I know that's stupid. But that's him. I've just left a phone message for our friend that I want out.

"Oh, and Jonathon, guess what I found this morning?... Out in the field behind the prison, I found evidence that Bent's been there, watching us.... A bunch of sunflower hulls in a place where I saw a reflection yesterday, like from glass—binoculars or a scope.... No, it's not a stretch. This guy chews them on every mission. And I was trained when protecting the president, whenever you see a glint where there shouldn't be one, there's danger....

"Yes. Left a message for her that I want to come home. I think I've done my share. I'll talk to her tomorrow and figure out how to do it. We'll talk tomorrow night. Maybe by then I'll be on a plane.... I miss you, too. And I love you."

The phone rang at ten o'clock, just before she went to bed. "Agent Mackie, this is Professor Conan."

"How the hell did you get a phone? You're not supposed to be making calls."

"I convinced them it's urgent. I need you to come out. I figured out what went wrong."

"Professor, it's ten o'clock at night. I'm not driving out there now. Just tell me what you figured out. I'll be there in the morning."

"Well, I'd rather talk face-to-face."

"You might, but I don't. Just tell me what it is."

"I think I can no longer be an alchemist," was his weak response, and she thought she heard him sob.

"I don't know what you mean," she said impatiently. "What happened?"

"I've gone back over the historical writings. The Emerald Tablet, the early alchemists' writings, Newton's journal."

"And?"

"And I rediscovered what I guess I already knew. An alchemist moves within the essence of the natural elements, adjusting them slightly, but always with respect and love."

"Okay?"

"I violated the soul of alchemy when I killed Linda Chavez. In defending my secrets, I killed her, and I killed myself as an alchemist. I'm also responsible for them killing Marge…. Two deaths…. I caused two deaths." Now he was definitely crying. "An alchemist must be pure, untainted. I am no longer such a man."

"Have you explained this to Perkins?"

"No. He's not here. He wouldn't understand anyway. He'd just accuse me of making it up."

"So what are you going to do? What's going to happen tomorrow?"

There was a long silence as he cried before finally speaking through his sobs. "You have to become the alchemist, Kathryn." It was the first time he had used her given name. "You, Kathryn Mackie, must be the new alchemist. You have to take over and continue my work."

"What? Are you crazy, Professor?"

"It's the only way. You know my secrets. You are pure, untainted by the hatred and crimes I've committed. I'll teach you, help you."

"And the fact that I'm a woman?"

"Makes no difference. You are like the moon, the mother of all things. The moon is as important as the sun. Alchemy favors no gender over the other."

Mackie was too tired to deal with these rantings tonight. She told Conan they could talk in the morning. She went to bed unsettled, her mind racing with what he had said.

❧

Mackie woke with a hand pressed over her mouth and cold metal in her ear.

"Be quiet and still, señorita. If you fight, I will kill you."

Hands grabbed her feet and arms and bound them to the bed with rope. Spread-eagled on her back, she closed her eyes and waited for the rape, the forced penetration, trying to relax as she had been trained, to avoid being torn and bruised. But the rape didn't happen.

"I will uncover your mouth, señorita, but if you yell, it will be taped shut."

The hand was removed and a light turned on. She saw two men standing by her bed. Both wore jeans and long-sleeved shirts that covered most of their dark skin. Their mustaches gave them a traditional Latino look. The one who had gagged her held a pistol pointed at her face. The second, at the foot of the bed, stood with hands clasped in front of his waist.

"What do you want?" she gasped as her eyes darted between them.

"We want to talk to you about Professor Conan," said the one at her head in heavily accented English. "In the morning, we want to talk with him. We will want you to take us to him."

"Why do you think I can do that?" she asked.

"Because you are his handler, señorita." He pressed the gun back into her ear. "Do not toy with us. We followed you here from the prison. In the morning, you will drive back and take us inside."

"He's heavily guarded. I can't get you in there."

The man pulled back the pistol and hit her twice, drawing blood on each cheek.

"I said do not toy! There are almost no guards, other than you. They will open the gate for you, and you will take us in."

She winced but breathed with some relief. They weren't going to rape her or kill her…at least not right now. If there were only two of them, she might have a chance in the morning. They'd have to let her drive.

"What do you want with Professor Conan?"

"That is not your business. You will take us to him, or we will kill you. We will still get to him, but it will be easier with you."

"I can't just let you go in there to kill him," she protested.

"I said nothing about killing him. We want to talk with him. Learn some things from him. Maybe even take him home with us."

The Cubans, she thought. *It's the damn Cubans. Still trying to get the gold.*

"You don't leave me much choice," she said.

Suddenly the man's face exploded and splattered bloody pieces across the foot of her bed. Then the other man pitched forward on top of her right leg. Within seconds, Michael Bent was cutting the ropes that tied her and pushing the dead body off the bed.

"Sorry to take so long, Kate. Had to make sure they were alone." He smiled tightly. "Hope this evens the slate, takes care of the one I owed you."

She took a deep breath and rubbed her wrists where they'd been tied. "Thought you did that with the car bomb."

He looked up, surprise in his eyes. "That was taking care of a partner, Kate. This was paying a debt." He looked at the two corpses. "Maybe you should call Perkins. I think he's good at cleaning up stuff like this."

"I'll do that, but first we have to talk."

"About what?"

"About why you've been watching us, and what you're planning to do."

She shook her head and smiled. "Jesus, Michael, you just saved my life! I'm sorry. What can I say? I should be thanking you, not questioning you." She began to shiver and pulled the sheets to her chin, where they turned red with the blood from her cut cheeks.

"Here, let me help with those cuts. They don't look too bad. I'll get some bandages out of my kit."

"Thanks, but first, before you leave, let's make sure these guys are dead."

CHAPTER 40

PHONING FOR HELP

"Yes, Mr. Perkins?"

"Got a problem, sir. It didn't work."

"What do you mean, it didn't work?"

"He didn't make gold. Ended up with a pile of gray shit just like he started with."

"Is he playing with us?"

"I don't know. I don't think so, but I've always thought this alchemy stuff was a bunch of crap. He's going over his papers tonight, and he'll try again tomorrow."

"I'm not sure we have that luxury, Mr. Perkins. I was about to call you. There's some heat building up here in Washington. I was hoping a success would help me cool it down, but if his gold-making isn't working, we might have some problems."

"What kind of problems, sir?"

"I'm not sure yet. Someone's poking around. Not sure who, but we have to cut our losses—"

"Just a second. I have a call coming in from Agent Mackie. It's awful late for her to be calling; better take it. I'll call you right back."

❧

"Little late for you to be up, isn't it?" Perkins greeted her.

"Yeah, but I had a bad dream that turned into a nightmare," Mackie answered. "Two guys—Cubans I think—are dead in my room."

"What? What the hell happened?"

"They tried to get me to bring them to the prison to visit the professor. Tied me up, hit me a couple of times, but they're now lying on the floor. Need you to clean up the room before morning."

"How in the hell did you pull that off?"

"It's a long story. I don't want to get into it now. Can you take care of this mess?"

"Yeah, I'll send someone over. Give me the room number, and wait till they get there."

"No way I'm staying here. It's room 305. I'll leave the door unlocked, but I'm not staying with these bodies."

"Okay. Where are you going?"

"I have a place. I'm going to try to get some sleep. See you in the morning, bright and early. Oh, the professor called before my visitors showed up. Says he might have figured out the problem."

"What'd he say?"

"Not now, John. I want to get out of here. I'll talk to you in the morning."

❧

Perkins called back the attorney general.

"Anything new from Mackie?"

"You could say that. She says two Cubans came after her in her room, trying to get her to bring them out to Conan. She shot them. They're dead."

"Oh, great. Now we have more bodies to explain."

"Sounds like it was quiet. No one knows. She wants me to clean it up before morning."

"You do that, and you need to do a couple of other things tonight. You and your guys need to disappear. Leave Conan there alone. This operation is over."

"What are you going to do?"

"Don't you worry about it. Call Mackie and tell her not to come in till nine in the morning. I'll have things arranged by then."

"What are you going to do, sir?" Perkins repeated in a measured tone.

"I'm going to cover our asses, John. You just get the hell out of there. This operation is history. Make sure you get rid of those two bodies. I'll do the rest."

"Mackie, Perkins here.… Look, sleep in tomorrow morning. I'll be tied up cleaning your room. We'll meet at nine. No need for you to be here before then."

She closed the phone and turned to Bent. "Perkins says don't come to the prison till nine in the morning." She shook her head. "I don't like it. Something doesn't smell right. Why's the son of a bitch suddenly concerned about me getting a good night's sleep?"

The Israeli sat on the sofa while she gathered her things. He had offered his apartment for her to sleep. "Because he needs time to get ready. That's why he's delaying you. And if we're finished here, I need to go. I also have a few things to do."

"Michael, I know you've been out there watching us. I know you tried to kill him." She stood in front of the Israeli. "You don't have to kill him. He called me tonight. He's lost his ability to make gold."

"What?" he blurted out. "What do you mean?"

"He says he tainted himself by killing that girl. That he can no longer be an alchemist. I was with him yesterday. He couldn't make gold. The experiment failed."

"But he still knows things," he said. "He still needs to be stopped."

"Michael, a lot of people know a lot of things. We know about your gold mine, Ophir. We know the secrets you're trying to protect. A lot of people in senior places know what's going on. Your killing Professor Conan won't accomplish anything."

He gazed at her. "Good try. I know you want to save him."

"Michael, you just saved my life. I'm not lying to you. I swear, the secret's out. We know Israel's making gold."

He crossed his arms. "Okay, so you're not lying. So he can't make gold any longer and we might have some problems. Why don't you and I just go home?"

"I think you should." She hoisted her bag over her shoulder. "Me, I'm going to get some sleep at your place and be at the prison at daylight."

"Why stay involved?"

"Because I don't trust Perkins. He's up to something." She hesitated, weighing the risk in telling what she knew. "And because Professor Conan wants me to be the new alchemist."

"What?"

"He says I'm pure and untainted. He says he can teach me to make gold."

"You want that, Kate?"

"I'm not sure. I'm really not sure." She smiled and gave a small nod. "But girls do like gold, you know."

CHAPTER 41
A LATE WARNING

"Jonathon, this is President Menton. I'm sorry to call you so late, but it's important."

He rubbed his eyes and looked over at his clock: 2:01. "Yes, sure, no problem. What is it?"

"I've had a friend in Miami looking into this Cuban connection. She just called me. Her message was that we have to protect Kathryn—quickly. I've tried to call her on the new phone, and there's no answer. Her old cell isn't turned on."

"Yeah, I know she doesn't keep it on 'cause she thinks they trace her with it," he mumbled absentmindedly, still half asleep. Suddenly jerking awake, he added, "What does she mean, protect her?"

"That's all she said. Probably all she knew. We have to get through to her."

"Well, send the police…or the FBI…to her hotel," he shouted.

"I did that." A pause followed. "She's not there, but there are two dead bodies in her room."

"Oh, Jesus," he cried. "Maybe someone took her!"

"Maybe. I just thought you might have a better number. I'm sorry to give you this news in the middle of the night."

"What are you going to do?"

"We're sending teams down—"

"From where?"

"Don't worry. We know they're clean. We have Marine special ops teams that'll be there first thing in the morning—both her apartment and the prison. We're closing this operation down. And I promise we'll find her."

CHAPTER 42
THE PRISON

Mackie drove up to the gate at six o'clock, a glow just starting to appear over the eastern horizon. She figured she'd have to wake up the guard to get the gate open. She had wanted to report developments to President Menton, but her new phone was dead and she didn't want to activate the old one.

That's funny, she thought as she drove up to the gate. *It's open, unguarded. What the hell's going on?*

She pulled her car as close to the gate as possible, got out, pulled her rifle case out of the trunk, and slung it over her shoulder. Once inside, she closed and locked the gate and hurried toward the professor's quarters. Her pistol was in her hand by her side. She realized she didn't have on the bulletproof vest that had saved her before. She thought about calling out but decided not to announce herself.

She found the door to his building also unlocked. No one was around. The place was silent. She wondered if she'd find the professor.

"Professor, wake up," she muttered as she looked around his room, seeing nothing out of order. "Wake up, God damn it."

Conan's eyes opened, and he turned to her. "Mackie, what're you doing here? It's early, isn't it?" He looked over to the clock by his bed.

"Yeah, it's early, but we've got a problem."

"What d'you mean?"

"They left you alone." She swept her hand in a circle. "Perkins and his guys have all left, and they left the front gate wide open."

"What does that mean?"

"I think it means they're expecting visitors. And I don't think they'll be friends."

"The Cubans?" he cried, holding up his mangled thumb.

"No, I don't think it's the Cubans this time," she said slowly as she peered out the window. "Took care of them last night. I think it's our own people…"

"What'd you mean, our own people?"

"I mean Perkins's people. Not really ours, although they claim to be."

"Is this because the pour failed yesterday?" He swung his legs to the floor.

"I don't know. What I do know is that you'd better get some clothes on and grab whatever you really need for this work—what we can carry. We need to be out of here real fast."

He looked bewildered.

"Professor, move your ass! Someone's going to show up and try to kill you. And if I'm here, they'll probably kill me, too." She jabbed him in the shoulder. "And I don't intend to wait around for them. Move it. Get your stuff."

He pulled on pants and a shirt and laced up his sneakers. He turned in a circle, panicking. "All the important papers are in the workshop."

"Let's go," she said, pulling him out the door. "To the workshop."

They raced across the central yard to the building with the workshop and rushed in. She started stuffing papers into a briefcase.

"The journal…and my laptop. That's mainly what we need," he panted.

"Okay, we got them," she yelled. "Now we're out of here." She dragged him toward the yard and the front gate.

"Shit!" she exclaimed as they left the building. "Look over there." She pointed to the west, where headlights were approaching along the access road. "They're here."

"What are we going to do?"

She took in the situation, pulled him into the building and dragged him to the large window they had installed.

"We're going out the window, the new one we built for you. Then out the back guard tower. We run for the tree line. If we get there before they see us, they won't know where we are. They're not going to spend a lot of time looking."

She climbed onto the bench and slid the window open, pulling him up behind her. First she threw out the briefcase and more carefully dropped her rifle case to the ground.

"Jump out. It's only about five feet to the ground." She helped him with a one-handed shove. Then she followed. "Wait, I want to close it." She pulled the window shut. As she closed it, explosions erupted at the front gate. "They've blown the gate," she yelled as she grabbed his arm. "They'll go to your quarters first and look there. We still have some time."

They ran to the guard tower, where she knew there was a door to the outside. It would be locked, but she had left her key above the door on her visit to the woods two days ago. She wasn't sure why she'd done that, but she was now glad she had. It was hot, even at the early hour, and she sweated while Conan panted.

"I can't keep up this pace," he complained, gasping for air.

"Wait till we get outside," she said, dragging him by his arm. "Then we really have to run."

It was two hundred yards from the tower to the edge of the cleared field. Fog still hung close to the ground, but it was only about two feet high. She knew they'd be sitting ducks if the intruders saw them, but she figured the group would spend most of their time inside, thinking Professor Conan was hiding after hearing the explosion. With a hundred yards to go, Conan sank to his knees. "I can't," he panted. "Go—take my briefcase. Leave me here."

"No way." She grabbed his left hand, pulled the arm over her shoulder, and stumbled forward. "God damn it, you have to try. At least move your legs. You have to help me out."

Mackie kept waiting for a bullet in the back, but it didn't happen. They made the tree line, where she dragged him into the brush and dropped to the ground behind a stand of palmettos. Looking back toward the prison, she saw lights and shadows, but it was deadly silent. She realized they had walked right under the tree in which Bent had perched and from which the panther had sprung. Looking up, she saw the branch was empty today.

On his back, sucking air, Conan grabbed her hand. "What do we do now?"

"As soon as you catch your breath, we're moving deeper into the woods. I know there's a campground, and the Interstate highway, about eight miles south. If need be, we walk eight miles and get help."

"What about your phone? Can't we call for help?"

She gave him a wry smile. "Unfortunately, they put a tracer on my phone. If I turn it on, it'll lead them right to us. So we're on our own till help arrives."

"Are we going to get help?"

"Yes, we will. Just don't know when." She got to her knees. "Okay, that's enough rest. Stay low, on hands and knees. We crawl till we get further into these trees. By now, they're probably on the tower with binoculars and scopes. Let's get further before the sun's fully up. If they don't see us, we're okay. We'll know if they start shooting." Patting him on the shoulder, she added, "Watch out for snakes and alligators."

She looked back and saw spotlight beams crisscrossing the field and pushing into the surrounding brush. "If that light hits us, freeze," she ordered. "I think we're too far in for them to see us if we're not moving."

Once, they were briefly illuminated. They stopped moving, and the beam swept away without stopping. In fifteen minutes of crawling, they were well beyond observation. It was daylight, and Mackie was sure the people in the prison would leave rather than search the woods.

Time was now on her side. The intruders couldn't stay around and risk having to explain their activities.

"You know, I think maybe we should stay right here rather than move south," Mackie said. "These guys can't stay at the prison for long, and there are people—good people—on our side who will be looking for me. I'm sure they'll come to the prison. You and I need to talk about what you said last night, about your future and whether I want to be involved in it. Whether I want to be the new alchemist."

"I'd like that," he said. "I'd like to leave some sort of legacy, some proof that I can do what I say. That I can make gold. I'd like to work with you, Kath—"

"Let's leave it Agent Mackie, Professor. We're not becoming buddies." She stared at him, waiting for a response.

"Yes, ma'am. Didn't mean to cause offense," he said softly and lowered his eyes.

They sat quietly for a few moments, the vultures complaining loudly about their intrusion, and the sun beating down. It was eight o'clock, but there was no morning coolness. Mid-June in south Florida didn't give cool mornings. It stayed hot all night, and daylight brought more heat.

She broke the silence. "Professor, you've said a couple of times that you were going to be the first alchemist; you were going to make gold but not destroy the world's financial system. I don't see how you were going to do that. What were your final plans, your end game? How were you going to avoid flooding the world with cheap gold?"

He sighed. "I had a plan. You might think I was naive, especially now, but I thought it would work. I had enough greed to want to make myself rich, but not filthy rich. Enough to be comfortable and independent. That's why I was selling to the hedge funds. Was that what got me caught, the hedge funds?"

She nodded. "Yeah. That and the Cubans. Still don't know what brought them in. Didn't you say they read something you published in a journal?"

"That's what Linda said. Anyway, my plan was to gather a group of distinguished people to witness what I could do. Nobel Prize winners, astronauts, great authors. People everyone would trust. Have them witness my work and announce to the world, with their confirmation, that I could transform lead into gold." He raised his arms. "At the same time, I was going to destroy all my notes and papers—maybe some sort of public burning—and announce that I would never do it again." He nodded slowly and murmured, "I thought it would be that easy."

"But you'd still know how to do it," she said. "And just like the Cubans, someone could force you."

"I said I was naive," he answered. "I didn't think of that. Now it's not an issue. I didn't know I could simply kill someone to become impotent." He paused. "Sorry. Didn't mean to joke about her death. I just didn't know what else to do with her."

"Well, I don't know what to do either, Professor. If I'm going to get involved in this stuff, you're going to have to explain more about the process. I'm not good at just following orders. And, by the way, what's with this Henry David?"

He shrugged his shoulders and smiled. "The name's easy to explain. Just a bit of youthful enthusiasm. In college, I read all of Thoreau's essays. He had a single-minded quest to discover the essence of life. Very much like an alchemist, even though he never wrote of alchemy. So I took his middle name—I became Henry David Conan. Never changed my name legally. Just started using it. Like he would have."

"And what about explaining this alchemy process?"

"I can try. But remember, I've been studying and working on this for years. I'm a physicist. No one before me has succeeded, although thousands have tried through the centuries. It's complicated."

She leaned over. "Try me. I'm a fast study. Just keep it simple."

Conan sighed, shrugged his shoulders, and pointed up at the sun. "That's the key: the sun. It's fusing hydrogen atoms together in a continuous chain of atomic explosions, creating helium and shooting out gamma rays. The solar heat and gamma rays have unique properties."

"So we're playing with atomic bombs here?"

"No, no, not at all. The explosions are on the sun. We're fusing lead and gold atoms together with the assistance of the sun's power. Put most simply, lead's atomic weight gets diluted to the lower atomic weight of gold—from 207 down to 196. At the lower atomic weight, it becomes gold; it is gold. By using the correct temperatures, timing, and mixture of metals, the lead turns to gold.

"Can I tell you why it happens? No." He spread his arms, his right thumb resting in the palm. "But it happens. That's about as simple as I can get."

A faint *whup, whup, whup* made them look to the east. It got louder, and they both shrank down into the grass, thinking someone was coming for them. The sound became a roar as three helicopters skimmed overhead, flying toward the prison from the east. Mackie turned to Conan.

"I think the good guys are here," she yelled over the noise.

CHAPTER 43
MISSING PERSONS

"There's no one here, sir."

"What the hell do you mean?" the attorney general yelled into the phone.

"There was a car in front of the gate, and the gate was locked, not open as you said it would be. We had to blow it. By the time we got to his room, he was gone."

"He must be hiding somewhere in there. You gotta find him—"

"Look, sir, we're already compromised. We looked everywhere we could, but he's not here. We're out of here before someone shows up."

"There's no one there, ma'am."

"That can't be so," President Menton protested. "The man's supposed to be guarded and locked up." She turned to her friend General Longley, who had pulled a lot of strings to arrange the helicopter rescue. "And Mackie's missing, too. Oh, Charles, did we wait too long? I'll never forgive myself if she's been hurt."

"There is a car here, ma'am. Pretty much blocking the front gate, which has been blown open. Just got a report back on the car. Rented to a Kathryn Mackie."

Longley grabbed the phone. "Captain, this is General Charles Longley. Mackie's Secret Service, one of us. If her car's there, she's there. She's a black woman, about five foot seven. You gotta find her. Either inside or outside. She could be hurt. You gotta find her, Captain."

"We're looking, sir. We'll find her if she's here. Wait, I'm getting a report of a woman and a man coming out of the tree line behind the prison. They've stopped. She's armed. She has knelt and assumed a shooting position—"

"Don't shoot her, God damn it, Captain. That has to be Mackie. She's defending herself and her prisoner. Let her know you're friends. She won't let you come close unless she knows you're friends."

"Kathryn, you scared a lot of people."

"Well, President Menton, I had a few scary moments myself."

"I'm sure you did. What happened out there?"

"It's a long story, but I think someone decided that Professor Conan had to go. A team showed up at the prison a couple of hours ago. They weren't friendly."

"Kathryn, you get out of there. Let the Marines take you back to Homestead. I'm going to get down there by tonight. And I'm bringing Jonathon. General Longley's also with me. He got the Marines in."

"Bit of a reunion?" Mackie said.

"You're darn right. And I'm going to try to get Hassie there, too. She gave us the warning that the Cubans were coming. Even though we were a little late." She paused before asking, "What happened last night, Kathryn?"

"I'll tell you the full story tonight, ma'am. First, though, the professor and I need to do a few things here.... Get his stuff together so it's protected and all.... What should I do with him?"

"Bring him with you. I'll have someone here to explain his future to him. From what they tell me, he's probably going to be a free man."

"Will the Marines wait for us? Might take a few hours, and we need to be left alone in his workshop."

"What are you doing? What could take a few hours?"

"I need you to trust me on this, ma'am. There are some things we have to do. I need to finish this assignment."

"I guess you've earned a few hours. The general will tell them to wait for you...and to leave you alone."

"Thanks. We'll see you tonight. And...one more favor?"

"What."

"Tell Jonathon I love him."

"That's an easy one, Kathryn. I think he already knows."

CHAPTER 44
THE NEW GOLDMAKER

After getting food and water and giving the Marines enough of a debriefing so they could look for the intruders, Professor Conan and Agent Mackie were left alone in the workshop. Cabinet doors stood open and tables out of position, but the room hadn't been trashed. All they'd been looking for was the professor, not his papers or equipment. To Mackie, that meant it hadn't been the Cubans or the Israelis. Her own people had come after Conan. She shivered as she surveyed the room and realized she might be making herself the next target.

"We need to straighten up before we get started," Conan said as he walked to his bench and reached to open the top drawer. "First, though, I put something together last night, once I realized someone else would have to take over."

He opened a drawer and pulled out the now dog-eared journal he had pilfered many years before, its brown leather cover blackened with age and handling. Then he took out a second, much newer three-ring binder. "This is my translation of Newton's journal," he said, holding up the binder. "Last night I tried to put into it everything I've learned, all the necessary steps." He looked at her. "I was up most of the night. Someone's going to want Newton's journal," he said sadly, placing it on the table. "Let them have it. But this…" He handed her the new book. "This you must never give up. It's more than a translation; it is a treasure map you must follow. It also has a built-in code I'll explain to you"—he pointed with his good hand—"and only to you. With the code, you will know everything I've accomplished. Without the code, nothing in the book works. Go ahead and look through the binder while I put this workshop back together."

Mackie sat and read. A few minutes later, she was interrupted.

"What's this?" Conan said, holding up a videotape. "It wasn't here last night when I left. Wait, there's a note. 'This is yours, Professor. It's the only copy. Do with it as you wish.' What do you think it is?" He looked up at Mackie.

She smiled. "I think Mr. Perkins left you a gift. I bet it's your confession."

He stood quietly, thinking, and shook his head. "Why would he do that?"

"Maybe he wasn't a total shit after all. Maybe he isn't the one who sent them after you this morning. If he thought you'd survive, he was making sure you'd control the tape. Remember, you did admit to some pretty horrible things."

"I'll just destroy it right now," he said, moving back to the bench. "I'll break it open and burn the tape—"

"Wait." She held up her hand. "Wait a second." Her fingers curled at her lips as she thought. "I'm not a lawyer, but that tape violated just about all your rights. You were tortured to talk; you didn't have a lawyer; you…claim…that you were forced to lie about the rape."

"Don't you believe me? After our time together, don't you know that I couldn't rape someone?" His eyes filled with tears. "You have to believe me. I just couldn't do that."

"Professor," she said, holding her palms out in agreement, "I tend to believe you. But I'm not who's important. Someone's going to consider charging you with murder. Someday you might want to use the tape to show how you were treated. I'm not sure anyone will believe a law enforcement guy did that to you. I can confirm most of it, but the tape is absolutely conclusive. If I were you, I'd keep the tape. Just as you told me not to let anyone have this book"—she tapped the open page in her lap—"you might want to keep it to yourself. Just in case. You can always destroy it later." She stood. "We need to get going on this. The guys outside don't want to stay around forever. I want to find out if I can do this. And one thing…"

"Yes?"

"I'm not doing this for wealth. I don't want to pour one of those kilo bars you were into. What I want is a little different." She walked to the bench and stood next to him. "Let me show you what I want to do."

He had prepared the lead the night before. Beyond that, he became an observer, answering questions and making comments as Mackie did the hands-on work. They couldn't wait till mid-afternoon, but he explained that the early-morning sun's rays had enough power; they just had to heat the metal longer.

Two hours later, after pulling the mold inside from the running water, she saw the yellow gleam she recognized.

"Professor, come over and look at this! I think I've done it! I've turned lead into gold."

CHAPTER 45
THE REUNION

One helicopter remained at the prison to transport Conan and Mackie to Homestead Air Force Base. Although under orders to wait until she was ready to leave, Kate could see the crew pacing impatiently in the field where they had landed, repeatedly looking at their watches. Finally, at about two o'clock, they were ready to leave. The flight was brief, and they were back on the ground before three. A man in a suit and tie was waiting.

"You two must be Agent Mackie and Professor Conan," he said, extending his hand. "I'm David Blume, special assistant to the acting Attorney General. We've had a few personnel changes today. New people at Justice and the Central Intelligence Agency. I'm with the new people." He held out a photo ID. "I've been asked to debrief you before taking you to your hotel. Some of your friends are there waiting for you, Agent Mackie," he added, nodding to her. "I have a room right here at the admin building." He pointed to a one-story concrete structure. "Could we talk for a few minutes?"

Mackie and Conan looked at each other. Mackie shrugged. "Sure. We probably don't have a choice, do we?"

Blume nodded. "I understand what you mean. You've both been through a lot. This is voluntary. If you want to walk away, you're free to do so. Neither of you is in custody. I think, however, I can give you some information that you'll find helpful."

"Then let's do it," Mackie said crisply. "Let's get it over with so I can go see my friends."

Inside was a small room with a table and four chairs. They sat.

"I mainly want to talk to you, Professor Conan," Blume said. "First, I'm going to give you your rights. You don't need to say a word here. I think you should get a lawyer, and you may walk out at any time. Do you understand?"

"I'm still here, Mr. Blume. Go on."

"I represent the federal authorities. We think you've been engaged in some questionable activities involving gold, and we think you have at least some involvement in the death of a woman whose body was found in the Everglades, near your house. There's also the issue of another dead woman found in your house." Conan started to speak, but Blume held up a hand. "Let me finish.

"We also think you've been mistreated by some of our agents." He gestured to Mackie with his hand. "Present company excluded. The bottom line, Professor, is that we are not going to press any federal charges. It's unclear whether your work with gold was illegal, but as long as it stops, we're not bringing any charges." He raised a finger for emphasis. "The dead women are another story. That's going to be up to the state of Florida to decide. Right now we don't think you're a suspect, and we're not going to do anything to make you one. The body from the Everglades is still considered a Jane Doe, and no one has come forward to claim or identify her. No one seems to think you killed the one in the house; it was the intruders. I understand there might be some sort of a videotape out there. We don't have it. If it surfaces, my guess is it might be the best defense you have." Conan turned to Mackie and nodded with a small smile.

"So that's about it, Professor. You're walking out of here a free man, and we'll get you back to your home in Fort Myers. But we really do want you to stay away from gold, sir. If you start messing around again, all bets are off, and we'll come down on you like a ton of bricks. Oh, one more thing. I've heard there might be an old book of some sort which you've been using." He lowered his eyes at Conan and pointed a finger. "We want the book, sir. It's evidence. We'll subpoena it if necessary, but it would be a lot easier if you just turn it over."

"Will I get it back?" asked Conan.

"Probably not. I don't see that you'll need it anymore, will you?"

"No, I don't need it. Does me no good anymore." Professor Conan pulled the ancient journal from a case hanging from his shoulder, gazed at it for a moment, and handed it to Blume. "Treat it with care, Mr. Blume. It's more than an old book. It uncovers wondrous secrets. In the wrong hands, it could do a lot of damage."

"So may I report that your work with gold has ended, sir?"

Mackie cleared her throat. "I'm going to answer for the professor on that one. Professor Conan is no longer going to have anything to do with making gold." She pointed at him. "Isn't that right, Professor?"

"That's right," he said with a grimace. "Couldn't even if I wanted to." He shook his head. "I'm back to being just a professor."

"I'm glad to hear that," Blume said. "I have transportation outside. We have a room for you tonight. Tomorrow, we'll drive you home."

As they walked out, Conan turned to Kate. "Will I see you again, Agent Mackie?"

She took his damaged hand in hers and looked at the bandage that circled his thumb. "Probably not, Professor. My job's done here." She dropped his hand then added, "But I do believe what you told me. I believe you couldn't have done it."

"Thanks…Kathryn. Thanks so much. That means a lot to me."

⚜

President Menton, General Longley, and Jonathon jumped out of their chairs and beamed at Mackie as she walked into the hotel suite. She melted into Jonathon's arms. Menton and Longley moved aside to give them space.

"Jonathon," she whispered in his ear. "I'm so glad to see you. Is it finally over?"

"It's over. I promise," he said, stroking her back. "That's why we're all here." He touched her bandaged cheeks. "What happened? What'd they do to you?"

"I think they call it being pistol whipped." She flashed a small smile through her tears.

She pulled back, wiped her eyes, and grinned at the other two. "Guess I'm not as tough as I thought."

General Longley shot back, "You're as tough as any goddamn Marine I ever met, lady."

Menton added, "Even the tough ones cry, Kate." She walked over and hugged her. "But let's stop the crying before you get me going, too. It is over, and we're going to tell you how it all ended. First, though, what happened last night? We thought we had lost you."

Mackie sat and sighed. "Is that chardonnay, my favorite chardonnay?" She pointed to an open bottle on the table. "Don't you think you should give a girl a drink before peppering her with questions?"

Jonathon rushed to fill a cup with the pale liquid as Mackie sank into a chair. She accepted the drink gratefully and took a long sip.

"Last night?" Mackie said as the others took seats around her. "Last night our Israeli friend Michael Bent saved my life. I think he was there to finish the job on the professor, and he saw guys following me. They tried to take me and were going to have me get them into the prison. I think they were the Cubans again. He took them out. Probably saved my life."

"We kept trying to call you," Jonathon said.

Mackie laughed. "Yeah, my new cell ran out of minutes, and I was scared to turn on my old one. Here," she said, pulling it out of her bag. "I still haven't turned it on. Let's see how many messages I have. I'll be damned," she exclaimed as she looked. "Guess who tried to call me last night?"

The others gave her blank looks.

"John Perkins. Late. After he had told me earlier to sleep in and be at the prison at nine. Here, let's see what he said." She put the phone to her ear. Her eyes widened in astonishment as she recited the message: "'Mackie, this is Perkins. Get out of your room. Don't come back to the prison. Watch your backside.'" She looked up at the others. "The son of a bitch tried to warn me. Whew. That's a surprise. He must have found his conscience.

"What about the attorney general? And the others?" Mackie wanted to know.

"The attorney general and the director of the CIA resigned this morning," Menton answered. "The attorney general tried to bluff his way through, but I understand that stopped once he was played your taped phone conversation. We're still not sure why they did all this. They're not talking much. It was certainly in our interest to catch this guy and stop him, but everything seemed done to help the Israelis. They wanted a quick-and-dirty—and very secretive—halt to the professor's gold-making activities."

"What about the president?"

"I don't think he was involved," answered Menton. "He seemed outraged and he gave no quarter to the other two. But I guess we'll never know for sure."

"Israel?" asked Mackie.

General Longley answered this time. "They won't admit anything, but it's clear they're making gold. Probably using the same process as Professor Conan. In some way, they learned of him, and they decided to take him out. Wasn't tough for them to insert Michael Bent into the task force. Actually looks like the task force was set up for them. As President Menton said, we don't know why so many rules were broken to help them."

"Were they going to take me out, sir?"

Longley's expression turned even grimmer. "It was certainly one of their options. I think maybe this guy Bent discovered the same conscience that Perkins found."

"And what about Mr. Perkins, sir? What's going to happen to him?"

"Maybe nothing other than an early retirement. As you heard when the professor got his instructions, we don't want a lot of publicity. If any of this gets out, there will be financial panic. Even though Professor Conan is stopped, any hint that someone can make gold will create international chaos. We need to keep the lid on it."

Mackie faced President Menton. "But the Israelis are still making gold. How's that keeping the lid on?"

Menton nodded. "You're right. These things move slowly, but I think we'll hear in a month or two that the gold vein in the Ophir mine is a lot smaller than first announced." She smiled. "They might continue to make their commemorative coins, but I don't think they're going to upset the world's gold supply."

"I'm still worried about the Cubans," Mackie said. "What if they come back after the professor...or me?"

"Agent Mackie," the general answered, "I promise that will not happen.

Our very special emissary, Hassie Chamoun, is in Havana right now. Otherwise, she'd be here. She's delivering the message that if there is ever again an armed incursion into this country, we will bomb their gold mine and their oil refinery first. Then we'll decide what to do next. They'll stay away."

They talked for another hour before Mackie reached into her bag. "I did bring you each a gift," she said with a smile. "Sort of a thank-you gift." She distributed three small cloth bags. In each was a gold coin the size of a quarter with an imprint of the sun.

"What's this inscription?" asked the president as she held it up to her eye. "Is that *K.M.?*"

Mackie nodded. "That's what it is."

"And today's date," noted the general.

"Right again," Mackie answered.

"Are they gold?" Jonathon exclaimed. "Made today by the professor? Is that why you needed a couple of hours in his workshop?"

"The initials are mine," Mackie said. "As I explained, the professor has lost his ability to make gold. But he taught me his secrets." She cocked her head and gazed out the window, fingering an identical coin hanging from her neck. "I made them. I'm the new alchemist." She smiled. "I'm now the goldmaker."

None of the others spoke for a moment, staring at Mackie with amazement.

President Menton finally walked over to her protégé, grasped Mackie's hands in her own, and asked in a quiet voice, "And what is our new alchemist going to do with her powers, Kate?"

Mackie looked her in the eyes. "I don't know, ma'am. There's so much going through my mind. I don't know what I'm going to do."

"That's a fair answer. You need time to think things over. I'm very proud of what you've done." Menton broke the spell with a clap. "And now, we should leave you two and let you have a proper reunion." She grabbed General Longley by the arm and led him to the door. "Let's have breakfast in the morning before we all go our separate ways. We'll see you at eight."

CHAPTER 46

BREAKFAST

A night of lovemaking and sleep and more lovemaking rejuvenated Kathryn Mackie. She and Jonathon walked into the cafe at eight o'clock, holding hands and glowing. The ex-president and the general were already seated.

They stood, and the older woman gave Kate a motherly hug. "You look much better this morning. And"—she pointed at Mackie's cheeks—"looks like you replaced those awful bandages with something less startling. Do the cuts hurt?"

"Not much," Kate answered. "Nothing compared to my chest after they shot me at the professor's." She hugged her boyfriend. "And Jonathon's a very good nurse."

Longley coughed lightly and pulled out a chair. "Let's have some breakfast, and then we can talk about your next assignment." He saw her startled look. "Don't worry. You'll like this one. President Menton has pulled another rabbit out of her hat."

Sipping her coffee, Agent Mackie gazed across the table to the other woman. "You're really not going to make me wait till after breakfast, are you?"

Menton smoothed the tablecloth in front of her. "I still have a few connections in Washington, so I talked to some people yesterday and called in a few favors. Bottom line, Agent Mackie, if you want, you're going back to the White House."

Mackie's hand flew to her face, which broke into a broad smile. "You mean no more chasing counterfeiters, no more running around the country after bad bills?"

"That's exactly what I mean. And as I recall, this young man"—she pointed at Jonathon—"lives in D.C."

"Oh, President Menton, thank you so much! This is the second time you've done this. I don't know what to say."

"We girls have to stick together, Kate. Now I can't promise what part of the team you'll be on. Might be president or vice president. But you'll be on the protection team. You'll be back doing what you did when I was there. They'll expect you in two weeks, which gives you some time to get things in order down here—maybe even take a vacation."

"Have you been talking to Jonathon, ma'am?" Mackie said with a laugh.

"We did have a few conversations about you. But he's a very discreet young man."

Menton clasped her hands on the table linen she had been smoothing. "I do have a question for you, Kate."

"Anything, ma'am."

"Have you given any more thought to gold?"

"Yes, I have." She looked over to Jonathon. "Actually, we have. We've decided that, for at least the time being, I'm going to stay away from gold. It's caused too much pain. I'm now into silver, President Menton...other than my charm." She smiled as she touched the gold coin hanging from her neck. "I'm not giving this up."

CHAPTER 47
THE VICE PRESIDENTIAL PROTECTION TEAM

Two weeks later, Agent Mackie was seated in the office of William McLaughlin, the chief of presidential protection in the Old Executive Office Building. Her wounds were fully healed. No bandages adorned her cheeks, and she was ready to go back to work.

"Agent Mackie," said the tall, chiseled man as he walked into the office. "It's been over a year, hasn't it?"

"Just about, sir." She shook hands with the man she used to work with. Now he would be her boss.

"No 'sir' for me, Kate. I'm still Bill. Glad to have you back. You keep showing up at unusual times without much explanation." He sat at his desk. "You've been in counterfeiting, haven't you?" He picked up her file.

"Until about a month ago, yes. A special assignment since then. I'd be interested in knowing what my file says about the last month."

He flipped a few pages, and said, "Not a hell of a lot. Says you've been in special counterfeiting training, dealing with coins and metals."

She smiled and nodded. "Guess that's close enough. I'm told there might be a position here for me?"

"Definitely. I think you know I was told to make an opening. But I have no problem with that. I know you do a good job. And now, with all that special training, you bring expertise in coins and metals." He shook his head and laughed. "What did you do this time to get special attention?"

She cocked her head and smiled. "I can say I got shot and pistol whipped. But I'm fully recovered and ready to go. Can't say much more, or they'd shoot me again."

"Always by the book, Agent Mackie, but that's the way it should be." He pulled over another file to review. "Look, I can't put you right into the president's team, but there is an opening with the vice president. I thought I'd start you there, and we'll see how things go." He drummed his fingers on her file. "That okay?"

"Bill, you're the boss. I know there was some pressure to get me here, but now I'm just another agent. Don't treat me any different, and I know you don't ask the others if an assignment's okay. Treat me the same as everyone else."

"Good. I'm glad we have that understanding. The vice president's going to Boston in two days to give a speech. You're on the advance team, and you'll be there for his appearance. Agent Larry Johnson heads his team. His office is down the hall. You'll meet with him and get integrated into his operations." As he stood to end the meeting, he said, "You grew up in Boston, didn't you?"

"Yes, sir."

"Maybe you'll be able to see some old friends or family."

As she left his office, she heard him take another call on his speakerphone and quickly punch the audio off. She could swear it had been John Perkins's deep, loud, and gravelly voice.

❧

The speech was to be at Faneuil Hall, the restored colonial meeting house across the street from Boston's monolithic poured-concrete city hall. The three-hundred-year juxtaposition was hard to miss, thought Mackie as she went through the protocol of checking manhole covers and rooftops. They even locked and secured the coin-operated sidewalk toilet, which was within blast radius of the speech site. She had no family left in Boston and few friends, so the trip was all business. She spent two nights alone in a nearby hotel. The team members were all professional and welcoming, and she detected no resentment over her sudden return to the protection service.

Her job entailed standing where the vice president's car door opened in front of the building's entrance. When he got out of the car, she would become a human shield between him and any attacker. She was in place when the limousine pulled to a stop, her shoulder holster pinching her still-tender chest under a loosely cut jacket. She scanned the crowd and the rooftops as she opened his door. The vice president swiveled on the seat to step out and dropped the speech papers he'd been reading, the packet falling to the pavement alongside the car. Mackie quickly crouched to retrieve the papers.

She heard the bullet slam into the steps behind her and felt pieces of concrete splatter against her legs.

"Shot fired!" she yelled as she rolled away from the car, her Glock pointing to the roof of the long building on her left. Someone pulled the vice president down on the back seat and slammed the door shut as the car sped away. Spectators sprawled on the pavement as three more agents appeared, carrying automatic weapons. Police yelled orders and scurried like mice toward the nearby buildings as Mackie pointed and yelled, "Has to be on those roofs. Came across the top of the car. Search those roofs!"

❦

The debriefing took place an hour later at the nearby police station. The vice president was in the air on his way back to Washington, the speech canceled.

"We were lucky on that one," said the team leader. "Two seconds later, he would have been standing outside the car. Can't find any trace of the shooter. We closed the area down within minutes. Had to have been a professional."

Mackie thought it through again. Had she missed something? Made a mistake? *If I hadn't gone after those papers, I'd have been standing. Would've hit me...* The recent events ran through her mind. *Was I the target? A professional wouldn't have fired before the vice president got out of the car.*

CHAPTER 48
WASHINGTON, D.C.

Mackie bought a Boston paper before flying back to Washington. Many of the articles revolved around the attempted assassination of Vice President Roberts. "A controversial figure," one article stated, "but never before the target of an assassin." Joshua Roberts was the firebrand of the current administration. A conservative ideologue in some ways, he was vehemently pro-Israel and pro-military but moderate on certain social issues. She hadn't yet said anything about her suspicions that she might have been the target, but she knew she would have to. From the airport, she took the Metro into the city and walked to her small condo.

She knew something was wrong as soon as she swung the door open. No chirping from her alarm system reached her ears. Dead silence greeted her. She turned the lights on and moved cautiously into the front room, pistol in her hand.

"Shit!" she exclaimed as she viewed open drawers and a bare tabletop which had held her TV. She'd been robbed. At least her laptop had been with her. She jerked in shock. The professor's binder! She had hidden it in the air conditioner vent in her bedroom ceiling. She closed her eyes, grimaced, and ran to her bedroom. Jumping onto a chair, she pulled down the access panel to the vent and reached into the area with her right arm. Finding nothing, she ran for a flashlight and stepstool to climb up for a more thorough search. She stuck her head into the opening and looked. "Oh my God," she cried. "It's gone."

She walked around in a daze and soon realized that the missing TV was a cover. Almost nothing else was missing. Someone had come looking for the book. And they'd found it.

"Professor Conan, this is Agent Mackie."

"Agent Mackie, I'm glad to hear from you. I wasn't sure we'd be talking again."

"Yeah, well, something's come up. Bad news. Someone broke into my condo and stole the book you put together."

"Not the book on gold?" he exclaimed.

"That's the one. I had it well hidden. I think they came looking for it. I'm trying to figure out who might have known about the book."

"Just you and I. And Blume's office."

"What do you mean? I was there when you talked to Blume. You didn't mention the book."

"You're right, but he sent someone out to my house a couple of weeks ago to check on me. I think they wanted to make sure I wasn't doing anything with gold. The guy put a lot of pressure on me to disclose everything, and I told him about the book. But wait, I need to tell you, someone broke in here, too."

"Jesus, Professor, I'm not sure what's going on. What happened there?"

"All I know is that when I opened my safe two days ago, the video was gone. I know it was in there. I put it in. Someone came in, opened the safe, and took the video. It wasn't broken into. Someone figured out the combination and opened it."

"Anything else missing?"

"No. Just the tape. That's all they took."

"This guy that visited you, how do you know he was from Blume's office?"

"He said so, and he showed me some sort of Justice Department ID. Had his picture on it."

"When was he there?"

"About a week ago."

"Before you found the video missing?"

"Oh, yeah, but I didn't tell him I had the video. He mentioned it. He asked about it. I told him about the questioning and that there was a video. I told him I didn't know where it was."

"Do you remember his name?"

"Let me look. I think I wrote some notes after he left." There was a pause as she heard papers rustling. "Yeah, here they are. Let's see…Bent—a Mr. Bent. That's who he said he was, and I think that's what the ID said. It was a picture ID, so I thought he was legit. Did I do something wrong?"

"No. I know Bent. I'll talk to him. But, Professor, if I can't recover my book, can you reconstruct it? Can you still explain how to make gold?"

"Maybe. With a lot of work. I don't have any of my notes or papers. I'd at least need Newton's Journal. You still have that, don't you?"

"No, I don't have it. You gave it to Blume, remember? Do me a favor, though?"

"Sure. What?"

"Don't talk to anyone else. No matter who they say they are. You call me if anyone asks you anything. Okay?"

"Give me a number, and I'll promise to call if I hear from anyone. This isn't the Cubans, is it?"

"No. The Cubans are long gone. You won't hear from them again."

"Every time I look at my thumb, I think of them," he said. "I also think of you a lot, Agent Mackie. I wonder whether you're ever going to make gold again."

"I haven't decided, Professor. But with the book gone, I guess I'll have to talk to you if I do."

Mackie had one more inquiry to make. She knew her old friend Hassie Chamoun had provided information and assistance about the Cubans. Hassie had come to Miami years ago as part of the Mariel boat lift, but her secret background as the illegitimate daughter of Fidel Castro had only recently been revealed. Her contacts with Cuba were strong. Chamoun was in Miami, practicing law and working as an elected city commissioner. Maybe she could do one more favor.

Kate sent an email:

> *Hassie, sorry I missed you in Miami. I wanted to thank you for your warning. There is one more thing. There's a mothballed state prison over in Hendry, the Hendry Correctional Institute, just outside of Naples, off of I-75. It's important for me to find out if it's really closed. A brief drive-by would answer the question. Do you know anyone in the Naples area who could do that? Needs to be quiet. Don't want any attention. Hope to see you soon.*

CHAPTER 49
A NEW ASSIGNMENT

The next morning, Mackie met with her new boss, Bill McLaughlin.

"Right back into the swing of things, Kate," was his greeting. "Understand you did a good job in Boston. The vice president is convinced you pushed him out of harm's way."

"I'm sure you've seen videos by now that show it didn't really happen that way, sir."

He nodded, gesturing for her to sit. "You're right. The film shows you bent to pick up his papers, then the shot. He wasn't out of the car yet. How do you figure it?"

She sat with hands clasped in her lap and looked across the desk. "I think I was the target."

"How the hell could that be?" he said, jumping up from his chair. "That's crazy."

"No, sir, it's not crazy. There are some things in my previous assignment that could make me a target. I can't go into it in detail, but I also had some papers from that assignment in my condo. While I was in Boston, someone broke in and stole them."

"So it's sort of like the fox guarding the henhouse, Mackie? You're supposed to be the guard, but you attract an attack because you're really the target?"

"Something like that, sir. I'm concerned that I'm attracting the danger I'm supposed to be guarding against."

"How can I find out more about this previous assignment? I need to know exactly what we're dealing with."

She swallowed and decided to take a chance. It was, after all, her life. "You might ask Perkins, sir. John Perkins."

There was a pregnant silence. He went rigid and stared at her. She clenched her fists and stared back.

"So you heard him on the voice box, didn't you?"

"Yes, I did. I'd like to know what the hell's going on."

"What's going on right now, Kate, is that you're off active protection details. Not because of anything you did. You've done nothing wrong. But I think you might be right. You might have been the target. We didn't think of that possibility." He shook his head resignedly. "Yeah, I talked with Perkins. I had to get some corroboration that your prior assignment wasn't going to be a problem. I got it from him. He spoke highly of you. Didn't tell me too much about what you'd done, and he never suggested someone might be going after you." He sighed. "I'm going to have to talk to Perkins again."

"So what do I do, sir?"

"You'll just have to work here in the office for a while. Administrative stuff. There's plenty to do. What about the break-in? Did you report it?"

"Yeah, a detective was by this morning." She hesitated. "Sir, there is one thing. Those papers in my place that were taken."

"What about them?"

"I didn't think anyone knew I had them. There wasn't anything wrong about my having them, but they're very important papers. Dealt with my previous mission. I didn't mention the missing papers to the police, and I'd appreciate it if you don't mention them to Perkins."

"Why's that?"

"I'd like to find out whether he already knows they're missing, sir."

McLaughlin, standing behind his desk, peered distractedly at some papers. His head yanked up. "You saying he stole them?"

"He might have. There's a lot about Mr. Perkins that doesn't add up. You do what you have to, but I'm sure I'll be talking with John Perkins again. I'd like to see if he knows about my missing papers."

"I'll see what I can do. My assistant will work out some administrative assignments with you. Oh, wait, what about protection for you? Are you still in some danger?"

"My guess is I'm okay now. If they could have killed me under the cover of a vice presidential assassination attempt, no one would have suspected it was me they were after. I don't think they want anyone to think I'm a target. Otherwise, they could have easily killed me in a lot of places."

"Who's *they*, Kate?"

"That's a question I'd like you to ask Mr. Perkins. I'm sure he knows. Tell him I don't appreciate being dangled out there as bait. I'd like some answers."

CHAPTER 50

THE VICE PRESIDENT

Mackie was going stir-crazy. For a week, she'd been analyzing after-action reports involving presidential security. Most were the result of someone reviewing video outtakes of presidential and vice presidential appearances. Every such appearance was taped, and every tape was reviewed to detect any security lapses by agents and to discover any suspicious persons in the audience. For the latter, sophisticated face-recognition technology was loaded with facial images of known or suspected security risks. She knew the work was important, but she'd never been happy with paperwork.

Her phone rang. "Agent Mackie."

"This is the office of the vice president. Vice President Roberts would like to meet with you at your earliest convenience."

"Oh, sure. Yes, ma'am. Whenever he wants. I'm at the Secret Service administrative offices right now. When would he like to see me?"

"I think now, Agent. Why don't you come over now?"

"Yes, ma'am. I'm on my way. Shouldn't take long to get to the West Wing."

"Actually, Agent Mackie, the vice president is at his residential offices at the Naval Observatory. He'd like to meet you there."

"Okay, I'll get a cab and be there as soon as I can."

"That will be fine, Agent."

That's funny, Mackie thought as she dashed to the restroom to make herself more presentable. *I thought he did his official business in his West Wing offices. Why's he dragging me over to the observatory?*

Thirty minutes later, she was shown into a large office at the vice presidential residential building. While in the cab, she had received an answer to her query from Hassie Chamoun in a short text message: *The facility continues to operate, although on a very small scale. The nearby convenience store says they're farming catfish rather than running a prison. Your friend, Hassie.*

Vice President Roberts stood up at his desk as she entered and walked around it with hand extended. "Thought it about time to personally thank you for your assistance in Boston." He grasped her hand with both of his. He nodded to the corner of the room. "I think you know John Perkins." She suddenly knew why they were meeting away from the prying eyes in his West Wing offices.

She looked at Perkins, who remained in the corner and raised his hand in greeting. Then she turned back to the vice president. "Yes, I know Mr. Perkins. I guess I shouldn't be surprised."

The vice president continued, "Agent Mackie, I was distressed to learn that your valuable service to us has disqualified you from the protection team. I brought Mr. Perkins in to explain the circumstances. You deserve better than a paper-pushing position. We've come up with a possible solution, a new assignment."

Mackie backed up a few steps so she could face them both. "New assignments with Mr. Perkins aren't exactly my favorite ones." She clasped her hands together at her belt and widened her stance. "In fact,

I'm surprised he's still with the government; thought he'd be in prison by now."

Roberts coughed nervously. "Let's not get carried away, Agent Mackie. Sometimes our people have to go a little beyond the envelope. Mr. Perkins has been very complimentary about your work. Why don't you reserve judgment till you hear what we have to say?"

"I'm all ears, sir."

Perkins spoke up. "Look, Mackie, I know we didn't always see eye to eye, but we did accomplish the mission. We stopped the guy. We're now talking about a new mission."

"And what's that, John?"

"We're going to ramp up the Hendry prison, start where we were when we were cut off by the Cubans and the Israelis. We're going to make gold for the United States Treasury. It's secure there, and we can provide you with full protection."

Mackie turned to the vice president. "Sir, it wasn't just the Cubans and Israelis who stopped us. One of our own teams broke into the prison to kill the professor and, as far as I know, to get rid of me, too. As I understand, an attorney general and a CIA director resigned once it was discovered that they were engaged in these unlawful activities. What's new now?"

The vice president motioned for her to sit next to Perkins, and he took the seat next to her. "What's new, Agent Mackie, is that we've gotten rid of the foreign influence and reviewed this program from the perspective of our national interests. At least one foreign country continues to make gold. It's a very valuable asset. We don't want to be left in the dust by this. If someday the world goes back on the gold standard, or even if not, the amount of gold we hold is crucial. The United States has always been in the lead—at the head of the line—in weaponry and finances. We want to stay at the head of the line. If someone's going to make and stockpile gold, it should be us." Shaking his head, he continued, "There's nothing unlawful about this, Mackie. We have as much right as anyone to make gold."

"And what about the international financial catastrophe when they learn what we're doing?"

"If I might interrupt, sir," said Perkins. The vice president nodded. "They're not going to find out. We're going to put such a tight lid on this that no one will know what we're doing. We're only starting down in Florida. Once we get the process going, we'll move it to a military base—out west probably—and it'll be as secret as the Manhattan Project was or Los Alamos still is."

"Why are you talking to me, Mr. Perkins and"—she turned her head and nodded to him—"Mr. Vice President? Please don't insult me by saying again you're just trying to get me some work."

"We know you're the new goldmaker, the new alchemist, Kate," answered Perkins. "We need you; the country needs you. We need you to go down to Hendry and get the process up and going again."

Mackie shook her head and stood, walked a few steps, and turned to them. "You only need me because, after stealing my papers and trying to start the process, you've failed. Hendry has been up and running for some time. And for all I know, you also need me because you failed to kill me in Boston. I'm tired of being lied to, stolen from, and shot at."

Perkins stood facing her, his hands raised. "Kate, we had nothing to do with Boston. I think we both know it was the Israelis. They're desperate to stop anyone else from making gold. We're going to protect you from them." His eyes darted to Vice President Roberts, and Mackie saw a small nod giving him permission to continue. "Yes, we have your papers. And, yes, we've tried to use them at the prison. They don't work, Kate." He pointed at her with a shaking hand. "We've followed the directions precisely. The goddamned process doesn't work. Doesn't make gold.

We need you to help us figure out why."

She smiled, remembering the error code Professor Conan had built into the papers. *They don't work because every damn number in the papers is ninety-six percent of the correct one—every weight, volume, and length of time. Close enough to not raise suspicion, but just a little bit off.*

"I'm not surprised you failed, John. Remember what the professor said: you're tainted because you don't believe in alchemy, just like he's now tainted because he killed the girl. I might be able to make gold, but you certainly cannot. Right now, however, I'm not sure I should even try. There's too much manipulation going on."

She swiveled to address only the vice president. "Sir, thank you for the opportunity to serve on your team. I will think about what you've both said. I'm just not sure I'm going to be able to help."

"It's for the country, Agent Mackie. We need that gold."

"Maybe, sir. Maybe we need the gold. But maybe the world would be better without this new gold. Maybe we're messing with nature too much. You can easily stop the Israelis with a couple of phone calls. Maybe no one should be making gold."

"She's a tough one," the vice president muttered after Mackie left.

"You noticed, sir?" said Perkins, shaking his head.

"I don't think she's going to help us, Mr. Perkins." The vice president walked to the windows and looked out. "We have any leverage over her?"

"I used some before, to keep her on the mission in Florida. But I'm worried about her connection with President Menton. If she brings Menton back into the mix, I'm not sure we'll survive. I don't think we're going to be able to force her to make gold."

CHAPTER 51
AN INTRUDER

Mackie was fuming when she left the vice presidential office. Why wouldn't they just leave her alone? She couldn't keep calling President Menton for help, but she was convinced these guys were all rotten. She wanted to call Jonathon, but he was out of town on business. She drove home, changed into jogging shorts and a tank top, and headed for the park to run off her rage and uncertainty. Roberts was, after all, the vice president. Was he speaking for the country, or were he and Perkins just the latest version of the guys who had been forced to resign?

As she huffed along in her blue NFL Patriots running shorts, she remembered that Jonathon, a Jets fan, hated the shorts and gave her a hard time when she wore them. Midsummer was hot and humid in Washington. She ran hard on a three-mile route, returning to her condo sweaty and out of breath. The alarm chirped properly when she entered. She punched in the code to disarm it then walked to the kitchen for water. She was in the middle of a swallow when she heard the familiar voice:

"Hello, Kate."

She swung around and reached for her belt before realizing she was unarmed.

"You don't need a weapon. I'm not here to hurt you."

Michael Bent, rumpled as usual, sat in a chair tipped back against the far wall.

"How the hell did you get in here? The alarm was on."

He shrugged. "Kate, I've dealt with many alarms. I need to talk to you."

"Why didn't you just call?"

"Because I don't like to leave traces. I'm not here, remember? I've gone home. Just give me a few moments and I'll leave."

"Do I have a choice?"

He leaned forward, hands on his knees. "We have a problem."

"I guess the hell we do. You're trying to kill me."

"I had nothing to do with Boston."

"So why are you here?"

"To explain what is happening and to ask you not to help them make gold."

Her eyes opened wider as she stared at the man. "I'm listening."

He stood and paced. "Israel is in trouble. It has a strong economy, but it needs aid and assistance from its friends to survive against powerful enemies."

"That's not new, Michael. It's been that way for years."

"Yes, but now our friends themselves are in trouble. We receive over three billion dollars a year from the United States. And you don't really have three billion to give away. Eventually there's going to be pressure to stop that aid. We have our unacknowledged nuclear capacity to deter a military attack. We need similar financial strength to stand strong without the assistance of others. We need the gold of Ophir. Just as gold built the First Temple in Jerusalem three thousand years ago, we need the gold of Ophir to protect us now. And as you know, our gold is only of value if no one knows we're making it."

"So you get on the Florida task force to try to kill Professor Conan, and now try to kill me?"

"No disrespect, Kate, but that's pretty small collateral damage compared to what's at stake."

"Now I'm collateral damage?"

"Come on, Agent Mackie, we all are. Soldiers are put in harm's way and sacrificed every day for the larger cause."

Mackie took a swallow of water and moved closer to the Israeli. "So why should you be able to make gold and not us?"

"We can keep a secret. America cannot. I guarantee that one of your people will talk. From the Pentagon Papers to the Wiki Leaks, your secrets always get out. It's inevitable. America's just not good at keeping secrets."

"So how did you ever get these guys to let you help chase down Professor Conan?"

He was silent for a few seconds. "Ever hear of the fifty-firsters?"

"The what?"

"Fifty-firsters. Group of officials in both countries who want Israel to be the fifty-first state."

"Of America?" She drew back in surprise.

"Yes, of America. We already receive your financial and military support. If we were to have an almost limitless supply of gold, we would bring a lot to the table. Adding a state isn't complicated—just takes a vote of Congress."

"But Israel's in the Middle East!"

"It's closer to Washington than Hawaii is." He helped himself to a glass from the cupboard and water from the fridge, emptying the glass in one long swallow. "We learned about Conan's new gold about the same time your Justice Department was forming the task force to find the source.

Israel convinced the people at Justice we could help by pulling favors from top American officials who are supporters of Israel. We were also able to supply an agent who specialized in making problem people disappear. As you know, that was me. They let us in. They didn't at first know about our gold; you started that pot cooking. Once Conan was found and stopped, your officials got greedy and decided they, too, wanted to make gold. They want a strong Israel—some of them want it to be the fifty-first state—but they also want to make their own gold. By doing so, however, they'll destroy our source and maybe the world's financial order."

He spread his hands. "That's why I'm here, Kate, to explain why we don't want you to help them make gold."

"Is the vice president one of these…these fifty-firsters?"

"You'll have to ask him. But he's made it clear he's going to run for president. He wants the Jewish vote. Wouldn't you think that's a good way to get it?"

"Jesus, Michael. You're telling me I have the future of Israel and the world's financial system on my shoulders?"

"You're Professor Conan's successor, Kate. You're the new alchemist. That power is immense." He shrugged. "What more can I say?"

"And what if I help them?"

"I leave today. My job is finished. Don't believe these people if they say they can protect you. Israel will not permit you to make gold."

She turned and looked out the window. "And how will you know my decision?" she said softly. "How will you know whether to kill me?"

He walked to her and gently touched the chain around her neck. "You wear on your neck the gold coin you made. If it remains alone, we will know you are making gold." He handed her a small chain with another coin. "This is the gold coin of Jerusalem I promised you. If you wear them together, we will know you have agreed not to make gold."

"And if I lie?"

"You will then be tainted, even worse than the professor. A lie of that magnitude, Kate, which would do so much damage, will destroy your powers. If you lie, I think you will be unable to make gold."

He looked at his watch. "I need to go. Here." He pulled a small cassette tape from his pocket and dropped it on the table. "Here's the tape I took from Professor Conan's safe. It's of no use to us. I can understand why he lost his powers. He did a horrible thing to that woman, even by my standards." He looked at her and shook his head. "How could you work with him?"

Mackie gestured for him to wait. "It wasn't quite as bad as you say. The whole video was scripted by Perkins. I'm now convinced he didn't rape her. He killed the girl because he learned she was a Cuban agent trying to steal his secrets. I'm not going to defend him, but I think you, of all people, shouldn't be passing judgment on me working with a killer. I was under orders—and a bit of blackmail—to work with him."

"I'm glad to hear that. And you are right; it is not my position to preach. After all, we were partners. Never want a bad partner."

Mackie stayed home for two days. Jonathon retuned from his trip, and they spent much of the second night talking.

"Jonathon, I'm going to quit."

"Kate, you worked hard to get where you are. Don't let these assholes make you give it all up. Just tell them you won't do the gold. Stay in the Service."

She walked behind his chair, placing her hands on his shoulders. "Yes, and do what? File reports every day? They'll never let me back in the protective service. If I refuse to play ball, they'll just leave me sitting on the bench. No, I have to get out."

He pulled her around the chair and stood to hug her. "What'll you do?"

"I don't know," she whispered into his chest. "I'll come up with something. I've saved some money…" She pushed back and smiled up at him. "Maybe I'll have to move in with you."

"That's a great idea. How about tomorrow?"

"That was a joke, Jonathon. But maybe some sleepovers?"

The next day, she handed her resignation to her boss.

Sitting at his desk, McLaughlin looked up in surprise. "What the hell's this, Kate?"

"I made a decision, Bill. A hard one. I've decided I'm just not cut out for this work."

He stood and walked around the desk. "I'm sorry it's come to this. You were a good agent. What's next?"

"I'm really not sure. Don't know what's out there for an ex-United States marshal and ex-Secret Service agent."

His eyes held hers for a long moment before he returned to his desk and pulled open a drawer. "There's a lot out there, Kate. You know about private military companies, PMCs?"

"Yeah, I think I've heard of them. Private security contractors. We used them in Iraq and Afghanistan, didn't we?"

"They're used all over the world. I think the best is—or was—Blackwater. There was a bit of controversy over a few incidents, and they're now called Xe, based right across the river in Virginia. I'm going to give you a name and an email address. You use me as a reference."

He smiled. "An ex-president might also be helpful, if you know one." He wrote on a paper and handed it to her. "Don't try to find their website. They don't have one. They keep a low profile."

As they shook hands, he saw two gold pendants hanging from her neck. "What are those?"

She raised her hand and rubbed the two coins between her fingers. "Memories of the past, Bill…and good-luck charms for the future."

That evening Mackie punched in a number in the 239 area code. "Professor Conan, this is Kathryn Mackie."

"Agent Mackie, good to hear from you again."

"Just want to give you a heads-up. First, I'm not Agent Mackie anymore. I've resigned from the government."

"Is everything okay?"

"Yeah. More or less. But second, I got your tape back from Bent. I can send it to you."

"You know, Agent—sorry, Kathryn, why don't you just destroy it. I want it out of my life."

"I can do that. And I have a favor to ask."

"Anything."

"I'd like you to do the best you can to reconstruct your notes on making gold. I'm not going to get the other papers back, and I'm not going to get that old journal, either. I know it'll be difficult, but I'd like you to try to do it now, while your memory's fresh. I'm not sure if I'll ever do anything, but if that day comes, I'll need your help. Will you do that?"

"I'll do what I can."

"And, Professor?"

"Yes?"

"Let's keep this between us. No need to tell anyone what you're doing."

CHAPTER 52
TWO YEARS LATER

Private citizen Kathryn Mackie sat drinking coffee at a sidewalk cafe in Mexico City. She had taken a position with Xe and was about to go on duty as bodyguard for a visiting State Department official. It was a typical assignment. She was thinking of Jonathon, who was pressing her for a long-term commitment. Mackie wasn't sure she was ready for that, and their relationship had become strained as he realized her hesitation. She was to meet her client at the elevator at eight. A headline in the newspaper on the adjacent table caught her attention. She pulled over the paper and read:

As anticipated, Vice President Roberts today announced his candidacy for the presidency. He dropped a bombshell, however, by making the keystone of his candidacy adding Israel as the fifty-first state. When asked about that position, he stated, 'We already support Israel with our military and our money. It's the most strategic location in the world. We need a presence in the Middle East. Israel has more natural resources than most people realize. Their Ophir gold mine is the largest producer of gold in the world. Israel as an American state in the Middle East will bring stability and peace to the region.

Those sons of bitches! Mackie thought. *He was up to his ears in the Florida operation. He knows the Ophir gold's fake. And now he wants Israel to be a state? She clenched her fists in anger. Wonder how many gold coins they promised him? I have to do something. I can't let them get away with this.*

Her watch beeped. Time to meet her client. As she stood, she skimmed the headline of another article in the paper: "Has Roberts been promised a quid pro quo for his fifty-firster position?" She saw the reporter was Benjamin Cohen. She headed toward the elevator deep in thought.

That evening she made a call. "Professor Conan, this is Kathryn Mackie."

"Kathryn, it's been a long time. Two years? What have you been doing?"

"Yeah, probably has been that long. I'm working for a private security company now. Still protecting people from the bad guys. Look, Professor, I never got back to you about your trying to reconstruct the formula for making gold. Were you able to?"

"Yes, definitely. I was surprised how much I remembered. I've put it all together, and I think it will work."

"Tell you what. I'm coming through Miami next week. How about if I drive over to look at the papers with you."

"Terrific. I was hoping you'd call someday. Just tell me when."

"How about next Wednesday? Look, if we were to do anything, how long would it take you to get the equipment and get set up?"

"The only thing I don't have on hand is the parabolic mirrors. They took them down to the prison, and I never got them back. Other than that, everything's easy to get."

"Professor, do me a favor. Order the mirrors. If we don't go forward, I'll reimburse you. If I'm going to do anything, it'll have to be soon—before the election."

"So what are you thinking about? Raising some money for the election? Some bullion contributions?"

"Not at all. Much smaller in scope. Remember those commemorative coins you and I made?"

"Of course. It was proof that you could be my successor."

"This would be some more coins. I'll bring a sample with me next week."

"How many would we make?"

"About a hundred, I think. But I'll know better when we meet."

"Kathryn, I hate to ask, but is this…legal? Am I going to get in trouble?"

"No one's going to bother you, Professor. In fact, this will get rid of all your worries. I'll explain it next week." She paused for a moment. "And remember how your last pour was close but not a perfect weight match?"

"Yes, and I think I can fix that…"

"No, Professor, we're not going to fix it. If we make these coins, I want them to be slightly off weight."

As Mackie disconnected, her hand went to her throat, where she still wore the two pendants. She lifted the Israeli coin over her head and placed it in her pocket. The hell with it," she murmured under her breath. "I'm going for it. But I'm not going to lie. I won't wear both coins and risk losing the power."

Although she was in the privacy of her own room, she looked nervously over her shoulder. *I wonder if they're still watching.*

CHAPTER 53
HATCHING A PLAN

Kate was always amazed at the thousands of different faces on display at Miami International Airport. It was a melting pot, and she heard Spanish, French and Japanese as she waited in line for her car. The large wheeled trunk by her side had made it through checked luggage inspection without a problem because of the coded label above its lock, which designated it as a law enforcement weapons case. Xe had connections, and she knew she couldn't have travelled with the case without the label those connections provided.

After loading the case into the trunk of the car, and her personal travel bag on the back seat, she followed the signs for I-75 west. The sun was behind her as she drove through the sea of grass Michael Bent and she had talked about two years before. *A long time ago,* she thought. A long time and another world. She saw a trooper and slowed. No free pass on this trip, and she sure as hell didn't want anyone inspecting the trunk. As she approached the only exit before the western toll booths, she decided to get off and drive to the prison. It would only take thirty minutes, and she wanted to make sure that the Hendry facility was back to mothballs.

The place was locked tight and empty. She was going to just drive by, but at the last minute she turned onto the access road and drove to the gate. A chain and padlock held it closed. She stopped and cut the engine, rolling the windows down to listen. The smell of hot, wet vegetation and dead silence surrounded her. She wondered if the panther still stalked the back wood line. The car moved slowly as she drove away and turned for one last look. It's where I first made gold. Let's see if I can do it again. One last time.

Professor Conan opened the door and waved as she drove up his long driveway. She had called him when she got back on the highway.

He walked to her car. "Kathryn, I'm so glad to see you. I thought we'd never see each other again." He extended his left hand, which she grasped with both of hers after she got out. "You were the only good thing in that horrible time."

"Yeah, that was pretty bad stuff, wasn't it?" She glanced at his right hand. "Not using it?"

"It's easier to just use my left hand. Tough to shake hands with a dangling thumb, and it turns people off." He shrugged. "This way, I just say I hurt my hand. Sort of keep it out of sight." He smiled. "Can't tell anyone what really happened, can I?"

"No. I guess not. Other than the thumb, how are you doing?"

"Fine. Fine. I'm back to just being a professor, and it's not bad. Since you guys didn't close out my bank accounts, I have some savings, and I'm comfortable. It is exciting to think we're going to work together on this project. Is it still on?"

"It's on, Professor. If you know how, and if I still have the power, we're going to make some gold." She looked him in the eye. "And if we can pull it off, we're going to shake some people up. They caused the problems we went through, and it's now payback time."

He raised both his hands. "You promised we're not going to get in trouble."

"There'll be no trouble, Professor. "We're going to get rid of the trouble. As I told you, I'm only here overnight. Let's go over everything, and, if you can be ready, I'll come back next week and we'll get to work." She popped the trunk and dragged out the case. "I'd like to leave this here if it's okay. It has gear I'll need, and I'd just as soon not drag it off with me tomorrow and then back."

"No problem. I have you set up in the guest room. You can leave it in the room.

Here, let me carry it for you."

"It's pretty heavy, and a bit fragile. I'll take it in, but maybe you could grab my suitcase from the back seat."

When she returned a week later, Mackie was glad to see the mirrors in place on the towers and water running through the filters behind the house.

"I've made a mold so we can pour ten coins at a time," Conan explained as he led her through his work area. "So it's going to take ten days if you need a hundred."

"I have two weeks off, so let's get started. First pour tomorrow?"

"Sure. Weather calls for bright sun, and I prepared the lead."

"You can do that?"

"Remember, I did last time, and it worked. It's the actual transformation that has to be done by you."

"Fine. I'm going to get some stuff out of the case I left to set up a perimeter security system so we won't be bothered…"

"Kate, you promised there'd be no trouble!"

Mackie sighed. "There's not going to be any trouble, Professor. This is a portable motion detection system that I always use when I'm on an assignment. It's easy to set up, and it guarantees no one can approach without us knowing. Just a precaution."

❧

"Look at these coins, Professor. They're perfect!" Mackie was shaking the first ten coins out of the mold, which she had just pulled out of the water. She grabbed another from her pocket and held it in one hand and a new one in the other. "Look the same to me." She handed them to Conan.

"What'd you think?"

"I think you're still the new alchemist, Kate. You've done it."

"I'd say we've done it, Professor. Let's see if we can do a second pour today. The sun's still pretty high."

❧

Mackie was dreaming of a truck beeping as it backed at a construction site when her eyes popped open. The beeps came from her laptop. She had powered it off, but it had been wakened by her security system. Someone was outside. Someone had tripped the motion detector. She jumped out of bed and padded over to look at the screen.

Jesus Christ! Someone's coming off the river. The camera in the detector she had placed outside showed a figure coming over the river bank and moving toward the house. Even with night vision enhancement, the picture was grainy and the figure hazy, moving stealthily and stopping every few feet. Mackie knelt at her trunk and opened it without turning on any lights. She pulled out night vision goggles and put them on so she could see—and choose her weapon. The floorboards creaked as she hurried to the front door. Turning the latch, she opened the door and went out. As she approached the corner to go behind the house, she remembered this was where she had been shot. At the moment she turned the corner going the other way. This time she moved slowly and headed away from the house to get a view of the back yard.

She knelt next to one of the mirror towers and swept the rear of the house with her eyes. There was the figure. Huddled down by the water trough next to the house, doing something on the ground. Mackie wasn't into warnings. Her training was to shoot first. But she wasn't comfortable killing without a warning, and she remembered that an alchemist could not take a life. She pulled her weapon from its belt holster and began to move closer. She knew she should get as close as possible—within thirty feet if she could do it undetected. Luckily the person was concentrating on whatever was being done on the ground and didn't sense danger.

Mackie aimed at the center of the back and pulled the trigger. Two probes with fifty thousand volts imbedded into the figure's back. She held the trigger of her Taser for almost ten seconds as the body writhed on the ground and screamed in pain. It's a woman; a goddamned woman.

"You roll away from that bundle or you'll get another shot," Mackie ordered. The woman did nothing, and she depressed the trigger, only three seconds this time. "Move your body or I'll do it again. If you prefer, I have a real pistol, and I'll give you a real bullet. Now move!"

The woman rolled to her left and away from the bundle on the ground. Mackie walked over and saw wires protruding from a black pack with something which looked like a clock next to the pack.

"I'd say you were setting a bomb, lady. Trying to blow us up. And now you're going to tell me why you were doing that …

"What's going on?" yelled Professor Conan from the window just above. Who's there?"

"It's me, Professor. I found someone messing around in your back yard. Everything's under control now…"

"The Cubans? Is it the Cubans?"

"I don't think so, Professor. But do me a favor. Go into that trunk in my room and get some cuffs. They're gray, plastic. I need them out here." She looked at the woman on the ground. "I'm going to secure this gal so I don't have to shoot her again, at least not right away."

Mackie used three sets of cuffs. On the ankles and the wrists and then a third set binding those two together. The woman lay on the ground bent almost in half with her wrists pulled down to her ankles.

"Now, ma'am, I'd like to know who the hell you are and why you're trying to blow us up."

"I have nothing to say."

"You want another stun? A real bullet?"

The woman turned her head and looked at Mackie. "I know enough about you, Agent Mackie, to know you won't do that to a defenseless person. When you removed the necklace, and came here to do your work, you made a choice. You knew the consequences."

The Israelis. "So why didn't Michael come?"

"He refused."

"I thought you guys couldn't refuse an assignment."

"We can't. He is now retired. I was sent. And that is all I will say."

"So what am I to do with you?"

Professor Conan had been standing behind her. Mackie took him by the arm and walked out of earshot of the woman. "She's not Cuban, Professor. I can promise you that. But she is here to stop us." She thought for a moment. "We have eighty coins, right?"

"Yes. Another two pours to get to a hundred. What was she doing?"

"She was trying to find out what we're doing," Mackie lied. "Probably sent by that guy Perkins."

"How did he know we were doing something?"

"Don't know, Professor. But my plan will stop him and anyone else from bothering us. Just have to speed it up a bit."

He looked at her as she thought. "Tell you what, Professor. We're going to stop our work, and I'll make do with the eighty coins we've made. The plan will still work. I'm going to leave after daylight. With the coins and with the woman. I want you to disassemble the gold-making stuff. Get rid of it. Then you need to take a short vacation."

"What do you mean, a vacation?"

"It's going to take about a week for me to get everything done. Until that happens, someone could show up to bother you. I think it would be best if there's nothing to do with gold here and better still if you go away for a week. Call me before you return. I'll be able to tell you if it's safe."

She patted his shoulder. "It's going to be fine, Professor. I promise."

"What about her?" pointing to the figure on the ground.

"I'm going to take her and drop her somewhere where they'll keep her out of our hair."

"He grimaced. "You're not going to…?"

"No, Professor. I'm not going to kill her. She'll be okay. Before dawn, I'll drop her near a hospital emergency room. She'll be trussed like she is, and she'll have a minor gun shot wound and an automatic weapon unlawful in Florida. Without any identification, and refusing to say anything, I'm sure she'll be held by the authorities for at least a day or two. That's all the time we need."

CHAPTER 54
THE PLAN, TWO WEEKS LATER

Benjamin Cohen, investigative reporter with *The Washington Post*, opened an envelope that had come in with his mail. A single page fell out, weighted down by a coin taped to it. A one-line message was typed under a long distribution list: *You should look into this.*

There was no signature.

"Another wacko," he muttered as he read the distribution list. *Eighty names. All around the world.* Then he realized he recognized many of the names as investigative reporters for major news media outlets around the world. He started to put it aside when he saw a name he knew. He picked up his phone.

"Maggie, Ben Cohen."

"Hi, Ben. What dirt you looking for today?" She laughed.

"Oh, nothing really. Just curious. I just got an anonymous tip, and your name is on the distribution list."

"The coin? You got the coin note, Ben?"

"Yeah, that's it. So you got it, too."

"I think everyone on the list got it."

"What are you going to do?"

"Guess I'm going to look into it, and I imagine the others will, too."

"So what do you think's the dirt?"

"I have no idea," she answered. "But it has to have something to do with the coin. It's a Jerusalem Gold commemorative coin. Maybe it's dirty."

⸎

"Oh, shit," muttered John Perkins when he opened his copy of the message. He saw his name was not on the distribution list, but the envelope was addressed to him, care of the office of the vice president. He knew postal security had delayed delivery to him. The message had probably already reached the named recipients. It had to be Mackie. *I should have closed her down when I could. Now what the hell do we do?*

Then he saw the postscript:

P.S. to John Perkins: Advise all interested parties that packets of information have been distributed which will be made public if any action is taken by you or others to pursue the authors of this communication. Make sure that Ishmael receives this message.

Perkins leaned back.

She's a smart bitch. We can't do a thing.

242

www.ingramcontent.com/pod-product-compliance
Lightning Source LLC
Chambersburg PA
CBHW020800250626
47155CB00003B/1165